Nip's Tale

Helen Armstrong divides her time between Wiltshire and Cumbria. She was brought up by the sea and spends her holidays on islands and coasts. She has kept animals all her life and loves hill-walking with her dog, bird-watching and being around horses.

Nip's Tale

Helen Armstrong

Illustrated by Ann Kronheimer

Dolphin Paperbacks

First published in Great Britain in 2004
by Dolphin paperbacks
a division of the Orion Publishing Group Ltd
Orion House
5 Upper St Martin's Lane
London WC2H 9EA

A catalogue record for this book is
available from the British Library

Printed in Great Britain by Clays Ltd, St Ives plc

ISBN 1 84255 106 X

www.orionbooks.co.uk

To Hetty and Lily

Nip's Tale

CHAPTER ONE

My name is Little Dog Nip. My teeth are sharp and my legs are short. My person, my human friend, is called Jeth. He has hard hands and a loud voice. He goes into people's houses at night and takes things.

There is another dog who lives with us. She is called Suky and she belongs to Tone. Tone lives in the same house as Jeth and me. Suky is thin and bony with wispy bits on her legs. 'My mother was a silky Saluki Hound,' says she. 'I was born to hunt gazelle across the desert but I am sure there is no gazelle in this town.'

One evening I have a question for Suky. She is stretched out on the floor fast asleep but that does not stop me. I nudge her with my paw until she opens her eyes. 'Suky,' says I, 'what do you think about it?'

She stares up at me, half asleep. 'What do you mean?' says she. 'What do I think about what?'

'Well,' says I, 'do you think it is all right for us to go into houses and take things?'

Suky sits up and blinks. 'Well,' she says at last, 'I don't go. Tone says I am too big.'

'Yes,' says I, 'but you know what happens. Jeth and Tone go into people's houses at night and take things and bring them home and then they sell them. That cannot be right you know.'

Suky says nothing.

'So what do you think Suky?' I say again.

'I do not think,' says Suky. 'We dogs should not think. It is not our job. We should do what we are told. That is easy enough.'

She is right of course. A dog must do what he is told, that is the rule. Thinking is for clever folk. I am not clever, I know. I am not clever, but I am brave, and true to my friends like a dog should be. That must be good enough. 'You are right,' I say at last. 'I shall try to stop thinking.'

So that is that. I try to sleep like Suky does and I try not to think.

Later on that evening, Jeth comes clumping past. He opens the front door and peers out into the night.

'It is good and dark out there,' says he to Tone.

'Going out, are we?' says Tone, 'Where to?'

'That old warehouse by the river,' says Jeth. 'The Watchman there is a silly old codger. He'll make no trouble, you'll see.'

I know what all this means. It is trip time. They always take me. I am a working dog you see. 'Our little watch dog. Sharpest ears on the planet,' Jeth always says. Now he looks at me and winks his eye. 'Ready, boy?' he says.

Then Jeth and Tone go off to get their thieving bag. The thieving bag is full of metal things. It clangs when it is moved. Then they put on their dark, soft thieving clothes and their dark, soft thieving shoes. They put dark, soft hats upon their heads. These hats are special. Later they will pull them down over their faces. I know this because they always do.

Last of all they put a little soft, dark coat on me. 'You must wear your coat,' says Tone. 'You are too bright and patchy. You shine in the dark and that will not do. You need your thieving coat my nippy friend.'

'Time to go,' says Jeth.

So out of the door we go, all three of us, into the van and off.

We do not go far. Jeth parks the van in a dark corner of a dark and empty road. Out we get. We are near the river. I can hear the water lapping at the road end. Jeth and Tone roll their hats down over their faces.

Then trot trot trot we go, close along a high wall. Trot trot, quick round a corner.

Slow and soft we creep towards a big, high door. Now doors are Jeth's job. 'There is no such thing as a locked door to our Jeth,' says Tone and it is true. This door is no different. One click, and another, then a heave and it's open.

Through we creep. Jeth, then Tone, then me. My ears are listening, listening. That is my job. I am listening extra hard tonight because this place is different. Most times we go to houses to take things, ordinary houses. Houses are easy beasy whether they are little or big. In the middle of the night they are quiet and still and I can hear everything, even if it is only someone turning over in bed.

But this is different. This place is so big, so high, so dark. Like a huge, empty garage, but bigger than any garage you have ever seen. Like ten empty garages. Like twenty empty garages. And it is full of creaks, and squeaks and the noise of the wind whistling under the doors.

I listen. And I sniff too. I sniff again. Yes, somewhere in this big, dark place there is a person. I smell it. I know it.

'That dog has noticed something,' says Tone. 'Look at him.'

My ears stretch to hear. I hear a click, and a shuffle. The sound is a long way off but clear as breathing. And with it comes the smell. The smell of a person, and the smell of tea and biscuits. A person in this building is having a cup of tea and a biscuit.

'The dog doesn't look too worried,' says Jeth. 'He must have heard the Watchman over on the far side. But that old man will not hear us. He is half deaf.'

So on we go. Jeth is looking for something. He has a tiny torch in one hand. It picks out metal stairs going up in the dark corner. Up the stairs we go. My claws go click click on the metal.

We reach the top. There is a little metal balcony and a door to one side. 'Through this way!' whispers Jeth. 'And Nip boy, you stay here! Keep your ears peeled, laddyo!'

He opens the door and they step into the room beyond. 'Aha!' says Jeth. 'Here it is.' His voice is whispery and rough. 'This is what we are looking for.'

I peer round the edge of the door. In the middle of the room is a big metal box. It has a big handle and a kind of clock next to the handle.

'My goodness me,' says Tone, 'what an old safe that is! It is out of the Ark I do believe.'

'Nice and old-fashioned,' says Jeth, 'and full of old-fashioned money too. That is what I like!'

'This should be a doddle,' says Tone. He laughs in a whispery sort of way. He reaches forward to the front of the safe. I watch, I watch too hard.

I forget to listen.

And then I hear a noise, very close! A door opens right below us.

It is the Watchman. He is not so stupid as Jeth thinks he is. He has heard something. He steps through the door at the bottom of the stairs. He is so close, I smell him in the dark. I hear him breathe.

Then Click! On go the lights. So bright that my eyes hurt.

I blink. I see the Watchman plain as plain. And he sees me.

'A dog!' he says. 'I do not think a wee dog has broken in all on his ownsome. Where are your friends my little pal?' Then he stands back and shouts up the stairs as loud as can be. 'Come out of there!'

There is a pause. A silence.

Then out comes Jeth. And out comes Tone. They come running out of the door of the safe room. They run across the little balcony. They run straight down the metal stairs towards the Watchman. They are both shouting. They swing their long arms. Wallop! Crash! They smash into the Watchman where he stands looking up. The Watchman falls backwards onto the hard ground. He lies still for a moment. Then he opens one eye. 'I have called the police,' he whispers.

Jeth and Tone stand and look down at him.

'Perhaps he has called the police,' says Tone.

'Perhaps he hasn't,' says Jeth. 'We will tie him up anyway. He has spoiled our fun tonight.'

So Jeth takes a scarf from his pocket. He ties the Watchman's hands behind him. Then he knots the other end of the scarf to the rail of the staircase. 'You are going nowhere,' says Jeth to the old man.

'We cannot stay here now,' says Tone. 'All the lights are on. Someone is bound to come.'

Jeth grinds his teeth. He looks like a dog who has lost his bone.

'Grrrrrr,' he says. 'I suppose you are right. Silly old fool,' he snarls at the man on the floor. Not so silly I think. He has stopped you, Jeth, and that was his job. Then Jeth turns to me. 'This is all your fault,' says he. 'You have let us down, you have! I'll deal with you later. We better get these lights off.' He flicks them off. Then off he goes through the dark warehouse, and Tone follows him. Tramp tramp go their heavy feet, out through the door into the street. I hear the van start up and go.

Without me. I have not run after them. I have stayed behind. So why is that?

I will tell you. It is because I am worried about the Watchman. He breathes all gaspy and weak and his eyes are shut. It cannot be right for him to lie on this cold floor. I lick his face.

'What is that, what is that?' he whispers to himself. He opens one eye and looks up at me in a wobbly sort of way. 'My goodness me,' says he. 'It is the little dog that I saw. I was not dreaming.'

7

He has both eyes open now. He is getting stronger by the minute. He tries to sit up. But his hands are tied and he is stuck.

'Wee dog, little dog friend,' says he, 'you can help me if you will. Could you chew at this scarf that binds me. Could you see what you can do?'

I trot round to his back. The cloth is tough. It is not so easy. I start to chew.

'Thank you for trying,' says the Watchman. After a moment he speaks again. 'I told a lie,' he says. 'I have not called the police. But I will call them as soon as I am free.'

I chew a little more. I pull. I twist. At last I hear threads tearing. The scarf falls into two pieces. The Watchman's hands are free. Slowly he gets up on his two feet. He looks down at me. 'Little dog,' says he, 'you are a good dog but you have bad friends. They will get you into trouble. In fact you are in trouble already. You should not be here you know.' He shakes his head. 'Be careful, small friend,' says he. 'I must go now. I have a job to do.'

He has his job. I have mine. I scamper off across the dark floor. I skip out of the door. I sniff the air for home and off I go.

It seemed only a short drive in the van but it is longer on my four feet. It takes me half the night to get home, but home I am at last. I scratch at the front door. It clicks open and here is Tone.

'He's back!' shouts Tone over his shoulder.

Clump, clump, here comes Jeth. He is as angry as can be. His whole night has gone wrong. 'You little pest!' he roars. 'Where did you slink off to? Out of my sight! You let us down you did. Hrrrumph!' snorts Jeth.

I scuttle in past his big feet. I hide under the table. After a while, Suky comes over to me.

'I was worried,' says she. 'I thought you might be lost or caught.'

'Not lost,' says I, 'but there was something that I had to do.' And I tell her.

She looks at me for a long while. 'If Jeth knew what you have done,' says Suky, 'he would be so angry. So angry.'

'I hope he does not find out,' says I.

But Jeth does find out.

CHAPTER 2

Jeth does find out. The next morning he is sitting at the table eating his breakfast and reading the newspaper. Suddenly he roars out like a bull. He throws the paper down. He leaps up and stares at me. His eyes pop with rage.

'It says here that a little dog let the watchman free! A hero dog it says!' Jeth snorts. He shakes his head like a mad thing. 'What little dog was that then? You little treacherous creep.'

He steps forward. His feet hit the floor like hammers. His arms flay like windmills. 'Come here!' he bellows.

I do not come there. I do not move at all. It makes no difference. He hits me anyway. It is not good to be hit. So I will tell you no more about it.

Afterwards I go and hide under the table. I lick the hurts that I can reach. I make no noise. At last I fall asleep.

Later that morning, Jeth comes stomping over to my corner. He peers under the table. 'Tone said you looked a gone pup,' says he, 'but you will be fine. You are tougher than that! I get a bit wild sometimes I know, but you don't mind it do you?' He laughs. It is an odd sound. 'Dogs don't mind a thump or two,' says he. 'It is good for them.'

He does not see that my front paw is hurt and he does not care. That is what I think.

Jeth stomps off. Suky noses over and sniffs me. 'Are you all right?' says she. 'He gave you such a thumping.'

'I am alive,' says I, 'but he is a cruel, bad man. How I wish I was not his dog.' I shut my eyes and lay my head down and try to sleep. I stay under the table for a day or two. Suky brings me bits of food and Tone does too, he is kinder than Jeth. I lie under the table and I think. By the third day I am well again except that my front paw is bent over a bit. And I have thought a lot.

While I stay at home, Jeth and Tone go out like before. They go out every night and leave me and Suky at home. Weeks pass. Nothing much changes for quite a while.

11

Then Jeth has an idea. 'This burglary lark,' says he to Tone, 'it is too much like hard work. Cars are easier than houses. We will pinch things from cars instead. And if we stick to cars, we do not need to work at night. We can have a nice lie-in. It will be better all ways up.'

'Anything you say,' says Tone.

'The little dog is fit enough now,' says Jeth. 'We need him to watch out for us. This can be a new start for him!'

I will be thieving again. That is clear. I am sure it is not right, but how can I stop now? Jeth will hurt me if I try to stop. So I go.

This time they take Suky as well. 'In daylight we need all the watchers we can get,' says Jeth, 'so we will take both dogs. That will be best.' The next morning we all get into the blue van and we go into the town.

Jeth parks the van. Out we get and stare around us. It is a broad road with big houses on one side and a park on the other.

Jeth looks hard at me. 'Nip, you are our guard at this end of the road. Do not mess it up this time or else!' He scowls at me and I tremble. Then he turns to Tone. 'You put that dog of yours at the other end. Then both you dogs, keep an eye out and bark if someone comes. Mind you do!' says he.

I do what I am told. I sit at my end of the road and keep a look out. I will do better this time. I missed the Watchman but I will miss no one today. While I watch and Suky watches, Jeth and Tone go from car to car, trying the doors and sometimes opening them and taking things.

Suky sits at her end of the road. She watches for a while. Then perhaps she dozes. She must doze, because suddenly there are two people coming down the road. A man and a woman. Suky has not barked at all.

'Whoops,' yelps Suky. And then she starts to bark as loud as she can.

Too late!

'Oy!' the two people shout together. They are shouting at Jeth. He is opening a car door with something in his hand. Tone is next to him. 'What are you up to!' shout the two people.

Jeth jumps back. Tone spins around.

'We're in trouble now mate,' says Jeth. 'I'm off!'

Jeth is right. They are in trouble. The two people are running towards them. They are closer now and I can see that it is a police man and a police woman. I know police when I see them and police are big trouble for Jeth and Tone. I know that. Jeth has trained me well.

Jeth starts to run along the pavement. Tone runs the other way, across the road. Suky runs after him because Tone is her person.

Jeth is my person so after him I go. He runs round the corner, into the park. And I am close behind him. Thud thud go his feet. Scamper scamper go my paws. And thud thud behind me goes the police woman. She is a quick runner, I must say.

Then Jeth puts one of his feet down upon a crisp packet. Up he goes into the air. Like a flying pancake.

And down again. Whump! He hits the hard ground, like a tree falling. He does not move much after that. The police woman blows her whistle.

After a while Jeth sits up. But it is too late. The police man is here too. And I see a big dark van pulling round the corner. It stops close by.

'Where am I?' says Jeth.

'You will be inside that van in a minute,' says the police woman.

'Umph!' snorts Jeth. 'I do not like the sound of that!'

'Get up,' says the police man. 'We can't stand around here all day.'

'This is all a dreadful misunderstanding,' says Jeth. 'I was not running away you know. I was jogging for my health.'

'You can explain it all to the magistrate,' says the police man.

Jeth gets up. He shakes his head sadly but he steps towards the van. Suddenly he sees me. 'Nip!' he cries. 'Do not worry little friend. There has been a mistake.' He winks at me as he speaks. 'Wait here for me like a good dog.'

'He may have a long wait,' says the police woman. 'The magistrate may not think there has been a mistake. He knows you.'

'But even so,' says Jeth, 'he has to have some

evidence.' He spreads his hands wide and empty and stretches out his pockets. 'What have I got here? Nothing! You will see, little dog,' says he, 'I will be back in a day or two, no mistake.'

I sit there on the wet pavement and look up at him. Jeth climbs into the van. Before the door shuts on him he says one more thing to the police woman. 'My dog is my best friend,' says he. 'It is good to know that he will always wait for me. He loves me whatever I do. A faithful friend. He will never leave me.'

The police woman looks at me. She has a kind face. 'I am not sure that you have been good to your faithful friend,' says she to Jeth. 'His paw does not look right to me. Little dog, you should come with us and we will find someone to look after you.'

I look at her. I look at her hard. But I do not want to go anywhere with Jeth. So I turn and off I scamper into the park. The door closes upon Jeth. The big van drives away up the road.

I am left alone in the green park. It is wet and cold. I stare a while at where the van went. Then I get up and look about for scraps of food. At last I find a sheltered corner behind a rubbish bin. I curl up tight. And then at last I sleep.

I sleep until I am woken by the scratch of paws and the sniff of a long nose right in my ear.

'Suky!' I yelp. 'How good to see you. But what a surprise! Where is Tone? Why have you come back?'

'I followed Tone,' says she, 'but he told me to run

off. He does not want me any more. He says he will go straight. I do not understand. What does he mean?'

I shake my head. I do not know either.

'Well,' says Suky, 'I do not see how he can go straight all the time. There are too many corners.' She is silent for a moment. 'I have no person now,' she says. She looks around and peers at all the shadows in the park. 'Where is Jeth?' she asks at last.

So I tell her what has happened. 'He is gone,' says I.

'What can we do now?' says Suky.

'I am not going to wait for Jeth,' says I. 'I have thought and thought about it. Jeth is a bad cruel man. I have been a good dog and a faithful friend. But Jeth is not a friend to me. I have stayed with him long enough.'

Suky nods her head. 'When I was a pup, my mother told me that we dogs should never leave our person, no matter what. But Jeth is such a bad man. I think you are right.' Her tail begins to wag. 'We can go together! I am glad there will be two of us. I do not like being on my own in these strange streets. I have been walking round and round. If I had not found you, I do not know what I would have done.'

I look about me. She is right. Everything is so strange with people walking here and there and never stopping. They all look so busy but where are they going? And who will stop and help us? No one, is the answer to that. We must help ourselves.

'What should we do?' says Suky.

'It is no good staying here,' says I. 'Maybe we should just start off and see what happens.'

Suky nods. 'What about this way?' says she, so off we go. She trots towards the corner of the park where the pavement is wide and crowded with people. There are lights on a pole; red, then orange, then green. Everyone moves forward and so do we. As we trot forward the people turn their faces and stare at us.

'This is not good,' says I. 'Someone will stop us soon.'

'I can see another dog!' says Suky. 'Over there! Oh and another one there!'

'Yes but they all have leads,' says I, 'and people on the end of them!'

That is the truth. There are dogs here, but they are not like us. They all have a person of their own. They look away when they see us and smile to themselves in a smug sort of way.

'I do not like this,' says I.

We dodge down a side alley. The yellow glare from the street lights cast shadows over us. We stand in the half dark, the two of us together, with not one idea of where to go next. Our ears droop and we shiver. We are a sorry sight. Then I shake myself. 'Suky,' says I. 'This will not do. When I was a pup, I was told that a little dog like me should never be frightened. I must be brave, like a lion, and fear nothing.'

Suky lifts her head and stands taller for a moment. Then she frowns. 'What is a lion?' she asks.

'I do not know,' says I, 'but something very fierce I am sure.'

Suky thinks for a moment. 'When I was a pup, my mother said that a Saluki like me should be swift as an arrow and let nothing escape me!'

'But what is an arrow?' says I.

'An arrow must be something very quick and very frightening,' says Suky, and then she begins to laugh. 'But really I don't know either!' Then we both grin our wide dog grins, with all our white teeth showing and our eyes gone little and crinkly in our furry faces. We laugh even though it is dark and cold and wet and lonely.

'Brave as a lion, and swift as an arrow, that's us,' I yelp and laugh, all at the same time.

'That's us!' barks Suky loud and clear. 'Brave and swift! So now, where next?' And her tail is wagging and her eyes shine.

'We must get out of this town and double quick. That is what I think,' says I.

'You are right,' says she. 'Anywhere must be better than this.'

She smiles her dog smile and we both stand up straight again and wag our tails and then off I run and she comes after me. We trot along the streets, side by side, my low shoulder next to her high shoulder. People stare but we do not pause. We do not wait.

We come at last to the edge of a wide wide road. 'Which way now?' asks Suky.

'Which way?' I mutter to myself.

'This way!' says a harsh voice just over our heads. 'This way!'

We peer up into the sky. High above, perched on a tall street lamp, sits a big black bird. 'Well, what are you waiting for?' he squawks. 'Come with me!'

CHAPTER 3

I stare up at the bird on the high street light. And the bird stares down at me. His feathers are black and glossy except for his neck which is grey like rain clouds. His eyes shine like green metal.

'Had a good stare have you?' says he. 'What a nosy dozy dog you are.' He turns his head to look at Suky. 'And you look even dozier, skinny friend.' Suky is staring up with her mouth open. 'When you've finished gawping I can show you somewhere to go for food and a safe bed. It is clear as my beak that you are both lost and going nowhere. Tell me I'm wrong!'

laughs the bird in a savage sort of way. 'Tell me that, my poor lost friends.'

'You are not wrong,' says I. 'We are lost and we have nowhere to go. But who are you? I have never seen a talking bird before! And you talk dog-talk too.'

'Can it be a bird, really?' whispers Suky next to me.

The bird hears this. 'Course I'm a bird,' says he sharply. 'I can talk dog-talk, people-talk, and any other kind you could mention. I bet you've never heard of half the speaking I can do, so there!' And he ruffles his feathers in a cross kind of way. 'But you are dogs, and you need food if I know anything about dogs. So follow me!' With two flaps of his sooty wings he lifts into the air. 'Follow me!' he calls out, then off he flies high above the busy pavement.

'What should we do?' says Suky. She looks at me.

'I don't know,' says I. 'The bird is right. We need food. We need a bed.'

'We will follow him,' says Suky. 'What choice do we have?'

So off we trot after the black bird. We keep one eye on him and one on the pavement ahead of us to see where we are going. But suddenly the bird seems to fall out of the sky. He plummets down so that his wings almost touch the heads of the people around us. He shouts to them! In people language. 'Frizzle's Circus! Come tonight. Best show in town! Best show ever!'

The hair on my back bristles with fright. 'Suky,' says

I, 'It is not right. How can a bird be so like a person.'

'A person in feathers,' says Suky and she shakes her head. She does not know what to think.

But the bird is flying high again now. 'Hurry!' he calls down to us. 'Hurry you two. No dawdling down there!' It is so strange to hear him. But hurry is what we do. And soon we arrive.

We arrive. But where?

It is a field on the edge of town. A field with a high fence round it. And in the fence is a gate. And over the gate is a board with big yellow letters saying FRIZZLE'S CIRCUS. A flag streaming from a tent-top says FRIZZLE'S CIRCUS, and 'Frizzle's Circus – get your tickets now!' shouts a red-faced man in a green coat by the gateway.

The man stops shouting when he sees the black bird and us. 'Oh Jackie Daw,' says he. 'You've had some luck there. Take them to Dingo. He will be pleased.'

'This way!' says Jackie Daw, for that must be the bird's name. 'This way!'

So that's the way we go. Between tents and painted caravans and metal caravans like long boxes. They are all crammed together close as can be. At last we come to a big blue caravan with high steps.

DINGO THE DOG MAN it says in high letters on the side. DINGO THE DOG MAN AND HIS DAZZLING DARING DOGGOS. I pause a moment. What is a dazzling daring doggo?

But here we are, so in we go.

Inside, a man is sitting at a table. He is tall and thin and his face is pale as a full moon. He must be Dingo the Dog Man. When he sees us he smiles. 'Oh Jackie Daw,' says Dingo Dog Man, 'good work!'

He stares at us for a long time. It is rude, I think. He has not said hello to us. I stare back. I feel the hair ruffle on my neck. He sees it. 'A bit cross are you, little dog?' says he. 'No need. You look just right. Jackie is a clever bird, that I will say. He always finds them out, the ones that will suit. The ones with no friends, for a start,' and he laughs. He laughs a long while and I think this is very rude indeed. I do not like Dingo Dog Man. At last he stops and looks at Suky long and hard. 'I don't know about you so much, my girl,' says he. 'Your legs are so thin. You are just too high and wispy. But never mind for now,' says Dingo.

Suky is cast down at this. She cannot help being so tall and thin. Her ears droop. There is a worried frown upon her furred forehead.

'Food is first,' says Dingo. 'I know dogs.' This sounds better. In a trice he puts two bowls upon the floor and fills them. He watches while we eat. When we have lapped up every bit of food, Dingo opens the door. 'Show them their kennels,' he says to Jackie. So Jackie hops and flutters down the steps and round the side of the caravan. 'This way,' says he. Behind the caravan is a row of wooden boxes with open fronts. 'This is your place,' says Jackie Daw.

'But other dogs have been here,' says I. 'I can smell them. They have only just gone!'

'Yes,' he says, 'two other dogs. They were here until yesterday. They left.'

'Left?' I say, 'What do you mean?'

'Mmm,' says Jackie. He peers at me with his cold pale eyes. 'They left because they did not like it here. That is the truth. They ran into the audience two nights ago. Someone took them home. It was in all the newspapers. Dingo was very cross indeed. Now he has to start again.' Jackie puts his bird head on one side and looks at me. 'Do not worry,' says he. 'You will be fine. You are so small and neat. It will be easy beasy for you.'

Suky is silent. She is not small and neat. She is tall and floppy. 'What will be easy beasy for Nip?' she asks. 'What does Dingo Dog Man do?'

'Not much at the moment,' says Jackie Daw. He chuckles through his black beak. 'He is a dog man with no dogs. But when he has a good dog he is a star turn. He is famous.' He turns his beady eyes to me. 'So you are called Nip are you? That is a good sort of name. And you?' he says to Suky.

'I am Suky,' says she. 'But what is this star turn? We do not know what you mean?'

'I will show you now if you like,' says Jackie Daw. 'Follow me!' He rattles his dark feathers and flaps his wings and soars up into the air. 'Go straight ahead,' he calls down, 'past that dustbin. Round that box. Now see that tent?'

24

It is not like any tent that you have seen. It is so huge. It is like a building, all lit up from the inside. 'That is the Big Top,' Jackie calls down to us. 'That is where we are going and this is our way in.' He swoops forward into an opening like a wide door in the side of the tent. Through it goes a sawdust track.

'But what is happening?' says I. 'The people over there are paying to get in, I can see them!'

'You are a dumb, dumb dog,' calls Jackie, 'but you will see soon enough.' He flies beside us through a kind of tunnel.

At the far end we find dark hanging curtains. With a flap and rustle Jackie lands on the ground beside us. 'Push through the curtains,' he whispers, 'but go slow and quiet. Keep to one side.' The curtains are red and plush. They are tied with golden cords and golden tassels hang on each side.

We push through. Everywhere is brightness and noise and dazzle.

'Here we are!' squawks Jackie softly. 'Now you see!'

In front of us is a round ring with a floor of sawdust, dry and smelling of wood. Lights glow down from high above. People are everywhere, in seats around the ring. Talking, pointing, laughing, eating, smiling.

'Oh Jackie Daw,' says I. 'Is this a magic place?'

'It is,' says he. His pale eyes shine. He chuckles in his throat and dances up and down in excitement. 'Wait and see.'

Just then there is a trumpet blast behind us. A drum begins to roll, quiet at first then louder, and loud at last as thunder. The lights dim into darkness. The people fall silent. I see eyes staring from every seat. Staring past me.

One more blast upon the trumpet and then – the crimson curtains pull back upon their golden cords. They pull apart and lift and through them steps a man in a high hat and a red coat.

'Welcome!' cries he in a voice louder than the trumpet. 'Welcome to Frizzle's Splendid Circus, the greatest show upon this planet. Welcome!'

He sweeps his tall hat off his head. He stands aside. Past him, past us, into the sawdust ring come all the brightest creatures in this world. Golden horses with pale manes and tails trot past us. Their golden hooves thud upon the sawdust as they pass. Jewels gleam in their manes and tails.

After the golden horses come two ponies. One is black and one is white. They pull a tiny carriage crusted with silver. Two cats sit inside the carriage, each with a silver collar. They smile and purr and wave their tails.

'Watch out for them,' says Jackie Daw crossly. 'They'd have your tail feathers quick as winking. Nasty things,' says he.

I stare on. What is this! A creature big as a house. Grey and huge. I tremble and I shake. Suky cowers down and shuts her eyes. The creature steps past on flat grey feet like soft cushions. I see grey ears like wrinkled sheets of mud, and a tiny eye that winks down at me.

'Who is that?' I whisper. 'Who is that?'

'No need to tremble,' says Jackie Daw. 'That is Grey Elephant and she is kind though she is huge. She is older than the oldest bird that flies. She is older than Red Coat Man. And cleverer too,' says Jackie.

I watch the wrinkled legs go past me and the tiny tail that dangles after. The people roar and shout. The noise makes my ears tingle.

Another trumpet sounds. Another roll of drums. Then through the curtains step people, people who shine with bright colours and gleam with silver and gold. The crowd cheers louder. Then come men in baggy suits, yellow and green. They tumble through the curtain, they fall, they hoot, they burst balloons.

'They are silly people, those ones,' says I to Jackie. 'Why cannot they stand up and walk about like other folk?'

Jackie clicks his beak crossly. 'They are clowns,' says he. 'Clowns. They are meant to do that.'

I do not understand but dare not ask. 'Watch now!' he cries suddenly. 'Watch now!'

There is a final trumpet blast. A final roll upon the drum.

The lights pivot and turn. They flash up into the high roof. The ring is all in darkness. The creatures and the people fall silent and still.

High in the bright space hang two shining figures.

'The Silver Twins,' whispers Jackie into my ear.

There is a crash upon the drums – and they fall! Fall. Into the dark beneath. But no. Even as I gasp, they save themselves. They reach out onto hanging bars. Then let go and fly again. Backwards and forwards they fly, weaving patterns in the dazzling air.

Then even higher, in the very roof's peak I see a shadow. A dark shape waiting.

A red spotlight swoops up and shines upon it.

Who is this? What can it be? What person has arms so long? What person has shoulders so wide? Even as I wonder, there is a great shout from the people in the seats below.

'Jezzaralda!' they cry. 'The flying ape!'

And here she comes.

Jezzaralda.

Tumbling and falling through the air. Swinging in giant leaps from one rope to another, past the silver figures. Down – then up again. Her arms reach wide. They never miss their hold. I hear the sizzle of the air combing through her flying fur. She swings. She somersaults. All that the Silver Twins have done, but faster, longer, wilder, stronger.

'Jezzaralda!' the people cry again.

Down she plummets like a thunderbolt towards the ring. She lands upon the dry ground soft as a feather. She lands close by where I stand.

Jezzaralda has long arms and short legs and a big head and red, red hair all over her. I see her square and furry back heaving with her breath. She made it look so easy but perhaps it was not.

The Silver Twins slide down their ropes and stand beside her.

'Jezzaralda!' the people cry again. They roar and clap and shout. Jezzaralda bows. She smiles with yellow teeth.

'The Silver Twins too!' growls a catty voice from the pony carriage. 'Do not forget them.' But the people have forgotten them. The Silver Twins bow but all the calls are for Jezzaralda. She smiles her yellow smile at the crowd.

Then she turns and smiles at the Twins. It is a teasing sort of smile. They do not smile back.

Suddenly she sees me. Her little amber eyes stare down at me.

'Oh little dog,' says she. 'So who are you? I have not seen you before.'

'I am Little Dog Nip,' says I. 'I work with Dingo Dog Man. I am proud to meet you.'

She nods at this. 'I wonder how you will like being Dingo's dog?' says she.

The crowd starts clapping loud again. Jezzaralda turns and bows and smiles. At last she trots off towards the red curtain. A small dark-haired person steps forward and takes her hand.

'That is Mary Anne,' croaks Jackie into my ear. 'She

looks after Jezzaralda and Grey Elephant too. She is a kind person.'

I watch the two short figures trudge away. Then I turn back to the ring. The show has begun in earnest. Each animal and person has a trick to do. I watch clowns and jugglers and horses and even Grey Elephant who dances so stately across the ring.

All this while Dingo Dog Man stands behind me and hisses into my ear, 'You too. You soon.'

Of course I understand now. I know what he means. I will do tricks like Jezzaralda and the Silver Twins and the golden horses and Grey Elephant.

I will be a star.

CHAPTER 4

The great circus show ends at last. The people clap and clap until they are tired. Then at last they troop away into the night.

I blink my eyes and turn to go. Suky stands close by. Her long face looks even longer and sad. 'Oh Nip,' she says, 'I cannot leap and fly and march and dance like all these animals and all these people. How can I live here? What can I do?'

'Maybe you cannot,' says I, 'but I can. I am quick and I am brave. I will work so hard – you will see. Then we can both stay here and be safe.'

'I hope so,' says Suky, 'but Nip, I do not think that

31

the circus is a safe sort of place.'

I stop at this and think. 'Maybe it is not a safe place,' says I. 'Maybe you are right. But it is a magic sort of place for all that. And maybe it is safer than it looks.'

'And maybe not,' says Suky. Then we both trot back to the kennels. It has been a long day. We curl up and fall into sleep and it is light before we wake.

Bang! Thump! Someone is beating on the kennel roof. 'Work time!' shouts Dingo Dog Man. 'Come out and get started!' he bellows. So out I creep. I stretch. I yawn. And out comes Suky.

'No need for you,' says Dingo to Suky. 'You are too tall and skinny.' Suky looks at him slowly then at me. Then she slips back into her kennel. Her worried eyes stare out at me.

'Come with me, little dog,' says Dingo Dog Man. 'I'll see what I can make of you. For a start,' says he, 'we'll have to hide that crooked paw of yours. People want dogs that look happy and well. That paw will not do.'

He leads the way into a tent which is full of boxes and clothes and hats and shoes and everything that you could ever think of. He opens a big chest and rummages deep inside it. 'This will be fine,' says he.

In his hand he has a spangled frilly suit with four legs. It looks like a sausage with bits on it. 'Stand still,' says Dingo. In one pull he has it over my head. And over my legs too. I am all wrapped up in cloth. It is so stiff and odd. Like bandages.

'It fits,' says he, 'I thought it would. You look grand. Those frills hide your paw perfectly. Off we go now.'

I do not feel grand. But I must do what he says so that he will want to keep us. I trot after him, all stiff in my suit, and follow him into the Big Top.

The sawdust ring is chill and silent this morning. The banks of seats are empty. On each side the tent is looped up. The wind blows cold across the wide space.

'No time like the present,' says Dingo Dog Man.

Off he goes. When he comes back he is dragging a set of boxes behind him, boxes and a tiny bicycle and a big round hoop of wood.

He leaves them on one side of the ring. 'We will start with basics,' says Dingo, 'and see how far we get. Sit!' he shouts, loud as a whip crack.

I sit. Of course I do. I am not stupid.

'Lie down!' he bellows. And I lie down. So it goes on. I can do all this. Of course I can. How much use would I be on a thieving raid if I could not behave as I should? 'There is no need to shout neither,' says I under my breath.

After I have sat, and lain down, and jumped up, and turned around, and stood still, Dingo Dog Man puts his hands upon his hips and stares at me. 'Mmmm,' says he. 'Better than I hoped. Now for the new stuff!'

He pulls out the boxes. He puts them like little islands round the sawdust ring. Between the islands he fixes ladders and bridges that he gets out of the biggest box. 'Now we will see,' says he. 'When I do this,' he waves one hand, 'you run to the next box and jump up.' I nod my head. 'When I do this,' he waves his other hand, 'you sit up and beg. Now let us try it.'

And so it goes on. Dingo waves one hand then another. He shouts and I run, I sit, I jump. I do all that he says. I run and jump and sit until I shake with weariness. Dingo is tired too. But he is very pleased. He smiles all over his pale face.

'My oh my!' says Dingo Dog Man. 'I do believe you are a little wonder doggyo. I do believe it. It will be Big Time for Dingo Dog Man now!' He smiles so wide that I see every tooth in his big mouth.

'I will go and have a bite to eat,' he says. 'We will try the difficult bits this afternoon.'

A bite to eat sounds good to me but Dingo has not thought of that. He remembers to pull off my spangled suit. He puts it on the top of a high box then off he goes. I am left sitting in the empty ring, all by myself, and hungry as can be.

'Hey you!' A gruff voice sings out from the shadowed seats. 'Hey you, little dog.' I turn and peer. 'I have a sandwich here – would you like it?'

I peer again. It is Jezzaralda. She is sitting upon the floor between the rows of seats and munching with her heavy jaws.

I scamper up the seats to reach her. 'Here,' says she. She hands me half a thick sandwich. I gulp it down with two snaps of my white teeth.

'Thank you,' says I. 'That is most kind.'

'We animals must stick together,' says she. 'These people do not mean to be unkind – perhaps. But they do not think.' She munches for a moment. 'You will be the best dog that Dingo ever had. You will. That is clear enough.'

'Mmm,' says I. I do not know what to think about that. 'He says we will do the hard things later.'

Jezzaralda looks at me with her little amber eyes. 'Do you fear flame?' says she. 'Do you fear fire?'

I think a moment. 'I do not know what fire is,' says I, 'nor flame either. Should I fear it?'

'You will see,' says she. She sighs a little and wrinkles her brown face. Her skin is thick and covered with tiny bumps. She has a tough face but her eyes are sad and bright and kind. 'The last dogs did not like the fire,' says she at last. 'That is why they ran away.'

I have nothing to say to that. I cannot think what fire may be. I shall see.

I sniff about a while amongst the empty seats. I find some crisps and bits of bread. I go back to Jezzaralda and lie next to her red furred feet. I snooze a bit. Then I hear a clump clump noise in the ring below. Dingo is back.

'I had better go,' says I to Jezzaralda. 'Will you be here to watch?'

'I cannot stay,' says Jezzaralda. 'It is afternoon now. In the afternoons people pay to see us animals in our cages. I have to go and meet them. But I will hear how you get on.'

'I will do well,' says I. 'I must do well. Then Suky and I can both stay here. We will have a home!'

Jezzaralda looks hard at me. Then she shrugs her shoulders. She turns and shambles off along the row of seats. She leans upon her knuckles as she goes.

'Little dog!' cries Dingo up the slant of the seats. 'Do not laze about up there. Here's work to do!'

Down I trot. In two shakes I am back in my spangled suit and ready.

It is a hard afternoon. Dingo goes back over all that we have done in the morning. Then he starts the new lessons.

The bicycle. How can I ride a bicycle? My legs are not right. My bottom is not made for saddles. My front paws slip upon the handlebars. And all the time the suit hugs me so tight that I can hardly breathe.

Dingo straps my back feet onto the pedals. He straps my front paws to the handlebars. 'Now run!' says he, 'move as if you were running.'

I know what he means. I have seen people on bikes moving their legs and rushing faster than I can run. People, but never a dog. It is not right for dogs.

I try. I move my legs slow. I cannot run just with my back legs. All my legs must move together. Suddenly the bike starts to move. How strange. I do not feel like Nip. I am just a creature tied up in cloth and strapped to a machine. My heart fails inside me.

'Good! Good!' shouts Dingo. He rubs his hands and smiles from ear to ear. 'You learn so quick! How famous I shall be!' says he.

'Now one more thing,' says Dingo Dog Man. 'Just one more and we are done.'

He unstraps me from the bike. He sets me down upon the floor. How good to feel the sawdust under my four paws! How good to run again.

'Just one more thing,' says Dingo.

I watch him. I am puzzled.

He fetches the big hoop of wood. He wraps the edges in a length of strange cloth. It smells so odd that it catches my breath. Then he sets the wooden hoop high on a box top, fixed by two clips.

'You see,' says Dingo 'all you have to do is jump through the hoop!'

He sets a low stool to one side of the hoop and a square box upon the other side. It is clear as can be. I have to run around the circus ring and jump onto the stool. Then I must leap through the hoop and down onto the square box.

I can do that. It is too easy to be true. That is what I say inside my head. No dog ran away because of this. There must be something more.

I am right. Dingo steps forward to the hoop. I hear a click. He had made a bright spark in his hand. He puts the spark to the hoop. I hear a rustling, crackling noise.

The hoop has changed. It is no more a hoop of wood. It is a ring of gold, of red, of flickering light, of smoke and scorching.

This is fire.

This is flame.

My skin runs cold under my fur. I pant with fright. I have not seen fire before – I do not need to. I know it in my bones. I knew it before I was pupped, that is how it seems to me. And I knew to fear it.

Dingo turns to me. 'Now once more my little pal,' says he. 'Just leap through there.'

'Just leap,' says he. 'Just.'

I must do it. That is plain. If we are to stay, if Suky and I both are to stay, I must do this.

I breathe into the bottom of my panting lungs. I lay my soft ears flat against the rough fur of my neck. I stiffen every muscle from my shoulders to my tail. I begin to growl. I growl deep in my chest. I growl at flame. I growl at Dingo Dog Man. I growl at all the fiery world.

Then I go. Like a bullet I go. Round the ring so fast that the sawdust flies up behind me.

Onto the stool I bounce with legs of steel. Up, up, high into the air.

I plunge straight at that flaming ring.

The brightness dazzles my eyes. The hot flames lick at me as I fly past. They feel out for my fur, my flying tail.

But I am through. I hurtle down onto the box. I

almost slip, so fast I go. Then down onto the sawdust.

I tremble in all my limbs. I stand and shake. I close my eyes to shut the dazzle out. Dingo steps over. I hear his voice.

'You are the best thing on four paws,' says he. 'I have never seen the like. Quick at learning. Quick at doing. Jackie Daw has done good this time and no mistake. But,' says he, 'we must sort out a new suit for you. This one is smoking just a bit. People won't like that. A flaming dog! That would be something! But people would not like it I know. We will get you a fireproof suit. That will be best.'

He pulls my singed suit over my shaking head. He is happy now. He hums under his breath. 'Dingo and his dazzling doggo,' says he. 'True at last. My oh my!'

And away he goes humming a little tune, with the suit over one arm. As he reaches the entrance he calls back over his shoulder, 'Food time little dog. Come and eat. You have earned it!'

I scuttle after him out of the wide circus entrance. But what is this straight in front of me? Jezzaralda is here in her cage. There is a big notice over her head.

MEET JEZZARALDA – ACE ACROBAT APE!
PAY YOUR MONEY HERE AND MEET
YOUR MONKEY PAL!

People are crowding round the bars of her cage. They have got bananas for her to eat. She reaches out

39

and touches their hands. She takes a banana here and there. She smiles her yellow smile.

Suddenly she sees me scuttling past. 'Hello little friend,' calls she. 'I am glad to see you.' The crowd pushes forward. Jezzaralda looks hard at me over their heads. There is a question in her heavy brown face. 'You did it?' says she. 'You jumped through the ring of fire?'

'I did,' says I, 'and I can do it again. I have to. But I fear the fire, I do. Dogs and fire are not meant to mix. I am sure of that.'

Jezzaralda nods her head in a thoughtful sort of way. She takes another banana. 'You are right there,' says she. 'And all us animals feel the same. But that doesn't stop Dingo, and people like him.' She shakes her head in a sad sort of way. Her visitors begin to call out to her and wave to cheer her up. So she lifts her head again and smiles her yellow smile. 'I will see you later,' calls Jezzaralda. 'I must look after my visitors. Bye!'

'Goodbye,' says I, 'I have my dinner to eat!' Off I trot to Dingo's caravan, then round the back to where Suky lies. In a little while Dingo brings two heaped bowls of dinner.

'One of you has earned this and one has not,' says he, 'but we will sort that out soon enough I'm sure.'

Suky looks up at him. Her face is more worried than ever. But Dingo says nothing more. He clumps away through the evening light.

The next day Dingo Dog Man brings me a new suit. It is like gold metal, very thin and very soft. It is much better than the first suit. I can breathe in it.

'This suit will keep those sparks off you,' says Dingo.

So off we go to the Big Top to practise, just like before. I run and ride my bike, and leap through the licking flames. That night, when I sleep, the bright flames fill my mind. I wake sweating with fear.

On day three Dingo comes to see me in my kennel. 'Today it is,' says he. 'Today you will be a real circus dog. Today you will be a star.'

CHAPTER 5

Today is my day, and evening comes at last. It is circus time. I wait close to Dingo in the dark tunnel. The red curtain pulls wide. It is all as before. The golden horses step through, then the pony carriage and the cats behind their jewelled window. The Silver Twins fly through the air above us and Jezzaralda flies faster and higher. The clowns somersault and tumble. It is all as it always is.

Until this moment now. Now is Dingo Dog Man and his Dazzling Doggo. That is Me.

Dingo Dog Man is dressed in brightest blue with

silver buttons. I am in my new gold suit. Dingo Dog Man steps forward into the sawdust ring. I trot next to him. The crowd stares and claps and laughs. Dingo Dog Man bows low. I bow as he has taught me. The crowd stares harder and claps louder.

Then we begin. The boxes are by the ringside. Dingo sets them out quick as quick. And off we go.

I feel the crowd sitting around us in the dark. I see their eyes glow. I hear their breaths flow in and out, in and out. The crowd is like an animal, out there, behind the bright lights. A big soft breathing waiting animal.

Each time I jump, the crowd murmurs. When I jump higher, the crowd shouts. So I jump higher than I have ever jumped before. The crowd roars. I run faster than I have ever run. All the people clap and shout.

Each signal that Dingo gives, I see it almost before he makes it. Each order he gives, I move almost before his whisper reaches me. His pale face starts to shine with joy. 'Oh little dog,' he whispers as I hurtle over a ladder by his head. 'You are the star of stars I do believe!'

I am. I am the star of stars. The crowd is on its feet now. The people cheer and shout. A hundred thousand eyes glow at me from the dark. The crowd is pleased. That is what counts.

And now, at last, it is time for the flaming hoop, the ring of fire.

'Now boy,' whispers Dingo Dog Man.

'Now,' I say in my heart.

The hoop flames into brightness. The crowd gasps. One or two or three voices I hear. They shout 'No! This is not right. The little dog will fear the fire. This is cruel.'

One voice or two or three says so. But mostly the people gasp and hold their breath. I start to growl, as I have done each day when I must face the fire. I growl. The sound rises up and fills the silence of that waiting crowd. I growl.

And then I go.

I run around the ring. I jump onto the stool. I leap into the fire and through it. I am safe in clear air beyond. I land upon the box. Then off I jump onto the ground and bow as Dingo has taught me. I bow even though I shake in every inch of me. I bow.

There is a silence for a moment. Then a noise begins. It is so loud it crashes down upon me, like thunder. The people clap and shout and bang their feet upon the wooden boarding of their seats. They howl and cheer and wave their hands and clap.

I bow and bow again and so does Dingo Dog Man. The crowd cheers again. I run around the ring and out through the red curtains. Out at last. Out of that noise into the dark night.

I run straight back to Suky. 'I have done well,' says I. 'We will be safe. We will be safe here now, you can be sure.' And then I shiver because I remember the flames.

'I heard the noise,' says Suky with a smile, half sad,

half pleased. 'I knew you would be clever at this,' says she. 'But why are you shaking, Nip? And why does your suit smell of burning?'

I cannot tell her. It is too bad for telling. But then Dingo Dog Man clumps up to the kennels and Red Coat Man and lots of others too and there is no time for talking.

'A little hero,' says Red Coat Man.

'A star,' says Dingo Dog Man.

'Hooray for the little dog!' say all the circus people.

Dingo takes off my golden suit. He brings us two bowls of food. At last the people go.

'What luck!' says Dingo Dog Man to himself. 'What luck for me. How rich I shall be. What a good life I will have now.' He pats me on my head but he is looking far away, into some place where he will be rich and famous. Then off he goes and we are left in the cool dark.

The next day Red Coat Man comes back. 'You are an overnight sensation,' says Red Coat Man waving a newspaper in his hand. 'We will put your name at the top of the bill, next to Jezzaralda.'

That is what he does. The crowds are bigger the next day and each day after. Red Coat Man is very pleased.

I am a star and that is that.

I am a star and so, each day, I join the parade into the ring. Each day I watch the Golden Horses and the Clowns, when they open the show. Each day I watch the Silver Twins and Jezzaralda and run into the ring as they step out through the curtains.

Each day I fear the flames more. My gold suit keeps me safe. I know it does. But I fear still. In the night, when I lie in my dark kennel, the flames flicker in my head. In the day I growl and tremble when I see them.

I do not tell Suky. She stays very quiet now and lies in her kennel all day. 'No one wants me here,' says she. 'If it were not for you, I would be thrown out quick as blinking.'

'They need me,' says I, 'so you are safe.' I try to shut the fire from my mind.

'I am safe, sort of,' says she. 'But I am nothing here. I can do nothing but lie in my kennel. This is no place for me. This is no life, Nip.'

'Perhaps you are right,' says I. 'But what can we do? At least we have food and a bed. It could be worse.'

Suky says nothing to that and after a while I trot off to practise.

All the circus people practise, every day. Each afternoon in the cold and empty ring, the jugglers hurl bright balls into the air. The clowns practise their falls and somersaults. The Golden Horses sweep around the ring while Red Coat Man waves his whip. High above, the Silver Twins swing and fly. They are not silver now. They wear striped tights and dark sweaters.

They all practise except Jezzaralda. She does not have to practise. She lolls upon the seats and peers up at the Twins. She bares her yellow teeth from time to time as if she was smiling.

The cats do not like it. The Silver Twins are their friends. 'That lazy monkey!' snarls one of them. 'She does not respect our friends as she should.'

'We will get even with Jezzaralda,' snarls the other cat. He glares with his yellow eyes and bares his sharp teeth.

One of the cats is grey, and fluffy like a baby rabbit. The other is golden, and smooth like a snake. They live with the Silver Twins. The cats are grumpy and so are the Twins. They are all grumpy together in a silver caravan on the edge of the ground.

The cats watch everything. In practice time, they sit upon the low ring wall and watch. And every day around the circus field I see them watching all that goes on. 'Those cats must see everything,' I say to Suky as I eat my dinner.

'Yes,' says Suky. 'They watch everyone. They know everything that goes on. They frighten me almost.'

'They cannot hurt us,' says I, 'but I am glad we do not have a secret or they would find it out.' Then I trot back towards the ring for the performance.

So it goes on. For one week, then for two. The people love me. Red Coat Man is happy as can be. We are safe. Or that is what I hope.

But I am wrong.

'Only two more days here,' says Jackie Daw one grey morning. He is sitting on a tent peg. The air is

47

full of mist. Suky has gone for a sniff around. I am watching the clowns clean out the cages. They are wearing dark blue suits from head to toe and do not look like clowns at all.

'Only two days?' says I. 'What will happen then?'

'We move on,' says Jackie Daw. 'We always move on. That is what a circus does you know.'

'I did not know,' says I.

'When we move,' says Jackie Daw, 'they will leave your friend behind. She is no use you know. They will not take her.' He blinks his cold bird eye. He lifts his clawed foot and scratches his grey neck.

I am still as a stone. I cannot speak.

'Well,' says Jackie Daw. He stares hard at me. 'What do you think of that?' says he.

'What do you mean?' I say at last in a whisper.

'Well,' says he, 'you will be all right you know. The crowds love you. So you will have good food and a warm bed for as long as you like. Look after number one I say. What is a friend after all?' He peers at me with his chill eye. He is so still I cannot see him breathe.

'Oh Jackie Daw,' says I, 'a friend is all I have. I cannot stay if Suky goes. We are together. That is that.'

Jackie Daw begins to smile now. He smiles so wide that his cold bird face is almost happy. 'I hoped,' says he, 'there was a true heart somewhere. A friend should be a friend,' says he. 'I have not felt so happy since I grew feathers.' He jumps and flaps and dances on the spot as if he were on a trampoline.

'You may be happy but I am not,' says I. 'We have been out in those cold streets, Suky and I together. We have been cold and hungry and lost and lonely. I do not want that again.'

'Well,' says Jackie Daw, 'it is your choice you know.'

'Yes,' says I, 'and easy made. Suky and I must run off before the circus moves away. We must!'

'It will be hard,' says Jackie Daw hopping a little on his grey feet. 'You will need someone to help you!' He bounces some more. Suddenly he opens his beak as wide as it will go. 'I will help you!' he squawks. 'I will! I will! I will!' At every word he bounces higher. At the last squawk he shoots up into the air like a black mop and tumbles back onto the grass.

'Well,' says I, 'help will be good of course. I do not know where we can go.'

Jackie is not listening. He is thinking his own bird thoughts. 'I have been a bad bird, little dog,' says he. 'I have helped Dingo Dog Man. I have looked for little dogs like you and brought them here though I knew he would be cruel to them. I can be better than that.'

I nod. Jackie has helped Dingo Dog Man, and that is not good, it is not.

'I am sure I can help,' says he. 'They will try so hard to stop you. You are the star now, Nip. You are money on four paws and everyone likes money.'

'I do not care,' says I. 'No one will stop us. I will go and tell Suky now.'

I trot off slowly, wondering how I shall tell her.

Then suddenly I see Suky coming towards me round the corner of a caravan. At sight of me she stops.

'You have bad news, Nip friend,' says she. 'I can see it from every hair on your back. Tell me quick.'

So I do. Suky sits down upon the wet ground and I tell her the bad news. 'We have to go, we have to run away,' says I. 'The circus will move on in two days. We must flee away before it does.'

Suky looks at me for a long moment. Then she nods her head. 'You are not saying why,' says she, 'but I know why. It is because of me. They do not want me. They will leave me behind.'

'That is true,' says I, 'but it is more than that, Suky. Each day I leap through flames for Dingo Dog Man. I did not tell you but I do. And each night I dream of fire, and I sweat with fear. That is not a life I want. I must go too. We must go together and go soon.'

Suky begins to wave her tail. She looks more happy than I have seen her for many a day. 'If it is best for you too, then it is not bad news,' says she. 'It is good news. It is the best news there could be.'

'You were right about the circus,' says I. 'It is not a safe place and Dingo Dog Man is not kind. He is as bad as Jeth. We will run away and leave it all behind. Jackie Daw says he will help us.'

'I am pleased if Jackie is on our side,' says Suky. 'He is so clever and can fly so high and see so much. He will be a true help.' Suky bounces off between the caravans wagging her tail.

As I watch her go, I glimpse grey fur and golden eyes. The fluffy cat is staring down at me from the top of the feed store. I shrug my shoulders and trot back to my kennel.

That afternoon we meet up, Jackie and Suky and I. We find a safe place behind the Big Top. Jackie peers over his feathered shoulder and makes sure no one is close by. Then he begins. 'There is just today and tomorrow left,' says Jackie. 'The circus will pack up on the last morning. You must be gone before then.'

'We had better go just after the last show,' says I, 'when it is dark. That will be best.'

'You must wait for Dingo to take your suit off,' says Suky. 'You cannot run off in a golden suit! And it would be good if we had been fed too. We may not find food for a while once we leave.'

'That is true too,' says I. 'You are right. When we have been fed we will slide into the night.'

'I will go now and fly around the countryside,' says Jackie, 'and see which way it would be best to run.'

We all three look at each other in the afternoon sun and we smile. Then a sound strikes our ears. A gentle pad of soft paw on grass. I turn my head. Here right behind us are the Cats. And close enough to hear every word.

Jackie Daw squawks. He is up into the air before I can blink. He flaps so quick it makes a breeze. He perches on a wire high above our heads. 'What do they want?' he hisses down at us.

'We know what you are plotting,' says Cat Number One. She is the fluffy one.

'We know everything,' says Cat Number Two. He is the smooth and golden one.

Suky and I say no word at all. We wait.

'We know you want to run away,' they say together. 'How angry Red Coat Man would be if he knew – and Dingo too! They are cruel when they are angry. But we will not tell – if you help us.'

'How can we help you?' says Suky almost in a whisper.

They turn their yellow eyes upon her. 'You must help us to get rid of Jezzaralda!' they hiss together.

'Get rid of Jezzaralda!' says Suky. 'What do you mean?'

'That monkey!' the cats hiss. 'She flies up there with our brilliant Silver Twins. She does all the things they do, but she does them better. She is a cheat!'

'How does she cheat?' I ask. I am puzzled.

'She is a monkey!' they squeal in their rage. 'It is all natural to her! She does not have to learn. It is not fair. No one takes notice of Our Twins. It is all that Jezzaralda! She must go!'

'What do you want of us?' I say last.

'We have a plan,' says Cat Two. 'A good plan. A clever plan. Look here.'

He pushes a tiny object over the grass towards us. He taps it with his velvet paw as if it were a mouse. It rolls a little then rocks to a halt. It is a tiny clock, jewelled, golden. It ticks like a small heart upon the ground. We stare at it. Cat Two looks at us. 'Have you seen it before?' says he. We shake our heads. 'Well this little clock is the favourite thing of Red Coat Man. He loves it so.'

'You have pinched it!' says I.

'Well yes, we have,' says Cat One, 'but it is in a good cause you know. We want Jezzaralda to be blamed for stealing it. We want this clock to be found in Jezzaralda's cage.'

'You will put it there,' says Cat Two. 'It will be easy for you, little dog. You are her friend. Then we will make sure that someone finds it, one of our dear Twins perhaps. Red Coat Man will think Jezzaralda stole it. No thieves in this circus! That is what he will say. He will throw Jezzaralda out double quick. Perhaps that nasty Mary Anne and the silly elephant will go too!'

They both look happy at this. They purr a little to themselves. Then they go quiet and stare at Suky and me. They sit so still they look like cats of wood or like the two china cats that sit on the Fortune Teller's table.

I am thinking hard. If I say no, they will tell Red Coat Man and Dingo about our plans. Dingo will chain me up. When the circus moves on he will leave Suky behind, alone in this cold town, and he will take me in my chains. All that is clear enough. But if I say yes? How can I trap poor Jezzaralda? I would be a cheating crooked friend. I cannot bear to think of it.

There is silence for a heartbeat or two.

'Yes,' I say, 'I will do it.'

CHAPTER 6

'I will do it.' That is what I tell the two wicked cats. I will help them to trap Jezzaralda.

Suky gasps. She draws away from me as if she fears me. The cats twitch a little. They are not sure, I can see. But 'Yes' is what I say. I stare straight back into those four yellow eyes until they blink. 'Yes,' I say again.

But there is 'No' in my heart. Dingo Dog Man has not chained me yet. The cats have not trapped me yet. There is time. There is a chance.

The cats look smug now. They begin to purr and wave their long tails. 'We knew you would see sense,' says Cat Number One. She shakes her soft fur like a fluffy cloud about her.

'We knew you would,' hisses Cat Number Two. He stretches his cruel claws in front of him. They slice the wet ground.

Then the two cats glance at each other. A tiny glance. It is a look that I am not meant to see.

And all at once I understand. They mean to cheat us as well as Jezzaralda. They are double cheats. They will wait until I have planted the clock in Jezzaralda's cage. Then they will tell Dog Man about our plans. We will be caught before we can run anywhere.

They will win all ways up. The Silver Twins and their Two Cats will rule the roost. Jezzaralda will be gone. I shall be a dog in chains, Suky will be left behind in the town, and I shall leap through flames for ever.

The cats rise to their soft paws. They turn to go. 'One more thing,' says Cat One. 'You must do it tonight. Then you will have no time to cheat us you know.' They smile again and purr a little and then they walk softly away.

I sit there for a long while. Then I remember Suky. I turn my head. She is looking at me with eyes so sad and puzzled. 'You will trap Jezzaralda?' she says. 'You will play their tricks for them? That is not right even to save me. I cannot let you do it. I will tell Jezzaralda.'

'Wait,' I say. I look around to make sure catty ears

are far away. 'I have this little clock, I do. But do I have to put it into Jezzaralda's cage? I do not think so. I am sure that you and I can think of somewhere better.'

Her eyes begin to shine. 'You mean to cheat them? Cheat the cheats?' she whispers. Her voice is so quiet that I have to lean to hear it.

'Before they cheat us,' says I. 'They mean to tell Dingo and Red Coat Man that we are running off, as soon as that clock is in the cage. That is their plan. I am sure of it. But we will have a plan of our own.'

Suky smiles for just a moment. Then she leans forward. 'I can think of how we can trap the bad cats in their own trap!' says she. 'Listen!'

So she whispers into my ear and I begin to smile all over my pointed furry face. 'What a good idea!' says I. 'But there is almost no time. Tonight they say! We will have no chance to talk to Jackie about which way to run when the show is over. We must just trust to luck.'

In the distance I hear the great gates of the circus pull open. 'Roll up! Roll up!' cries Red Coat Man, 'Frizzle's Famous Circus!'

I hop from paw to paw. 'We must hurry,' says I.

'You must let the cats see you put the clock in Jezzaralda's cage. That is the first thing,' says Suky. 'You must pretend.'

I lift the tiny clock gently with my teeth. I let it roll back into my mouth.

'To Jezzaralda's cage,' I mumble through the clock. 'Let's go.'

We trot together over the wide circus ground. I feel the cats' eyes upon me as we run. I turn my head. I see them. The light is fading as evening draws on but still I see them. Cat One is under the ice cream van. Cat Two is cleaning his smooth fur by Dingo's caravan. Neither looks my way. But both see me, I know that.

On we trot towards the Big Top. We go to Jezzaralda's cage. Jezzaralda is warming up. She is stretching and bending and she sees us in mid-stretch. 'Dear friends,' says she, 'there is no time to talk now. I shall be in the ring very soon.'

'Jezzaralda,' I mumble through my full and ticking mouth. She stares at me. 'Please do not stare so Jezzaralda. Pretend to talk to Suky. Please.'

She is an ape you know. They are a clever tribe. She rolls her big head slow and gentle in a circle as if she was stretching her neck. Then she smiles at Suky. Her yellow teeth flash.

'Dear Suk,' says she, 'how nice of you to come and wish me luck.' She bends forward and stretches her long arms down and then up. As she moves I see her small eyes scan and seek. I see the moment when she finds Cat One and then Cat Two. 'I see two creatures who are no friends of mine,' she whispers into the straw as she bends. 'But no questions now I think.' Then she pulls up and stretches to the ceiling of her cage.

'May I jump into your cage Jezzaralda friend?' I mumble.

'If you need to,' says she. She wants to ask. I see she does. But she only nods and smiles. And then she turns her back and starts to chat to Suky.

Up I leap onto the rim of the cage. I push between the rusty bars. I look over one shoulder. The cats are closer now. I see four yellow eyes glow in the half light. I step forward and bend my head into the straw. I make a sort of sicky noise. It is not nice I know but I hope the cats hear it. I push my nose right into the heap of straw. I drop the clock. Just for a second it lies there ticking its heart-sound up at me. Then I flick out my tongue and pull it back into my mouth.

'You are poorly Nip,' says Jezzaralda, 'I wish I knew why. I shall want to hear the whole story,' and her eyes gleam down at me.

Then there is a clang. The door of the cage swings open. It is Mary Anne come to get Jezzaralda. She is smiling as she always does. 'It is your call soon Jezzaralda,' says Mary Anne. 'And Nip, you must run now. Dingo Dog Man is looking for you. Off you go little dog. Come, Jezzaralda, come and be brushed.' Jezzaralda goes out through the door and down the steps.

I leap from the cage. I run off into the half dark. The clock tick ticks in my mouth. Behind me I hear Suky's paws upon the grass.

'This way,' I hiss. I skid around one corner then another. We are late for Dingo Dog Man. I hope the cats will think we are running to get back to him. But we are not. I take a sideways turn and then another. We are at the Silver Caravan. Inside I see the Twins setting their silver crowns upon their silver hair.

'Look there!' says Suky softly. 'Under the caravan. There are the bowls I told you about!'

Under the caravan gleam two cat bowls. One is silver, one is gold. I stretch my neck under the floor of the caravan. I flick one of the bowls with my nose. I tilt it. I drop the clock beneath the bowl. It is out of sight. All is as it was before.

Tick Tock goes the clock. It echoes in its metal cave.

'They will hear it!' says Suky.

'Not now,' says I. 'Now is Show Time!'

With a quick leap I'm off again. Suky is after me swifter than the wind. As we reach our kennels I hear the door of the Silver Caravan crash open. The Twins are on their way.

And here comes Dingo Dog Man. His face is paler than milk. 'Oh little dog,' he says, 'you frightened me. I thought you'd lost yourself. What a pickle I would be in then, to be sure. Now hurry!'

So into my gold suit I leap. Suky crawls into her dark kennel and closes her eyes. Off I go with Dingo Dog Man.

The parade is lining up by the Big Tent. Something is wrong. 'What is the matter?' I hiss up at Grey Elephant's huge ear.

She blinks her tiny eye. 'It is Red Coat Man,' says she.

'What a temper he is in. He says he has lost the Time.'

'Ah,' says I. Just then I hear a stamping noise. Here is Red Coat Man. His face is as red as his coat. He cracks his whip over our heads. He stamps his shiny boots into the grass.

'One of you is a wicked thief!' cries he. 'One of you has took my clock. My little ticking friend. My long time pal.' He looks about at everyone of us. 'Who is it?' he roars.

Well no one speaks. Of course. The cats purr just a little. They brush their long whiskers with their soft paws. They say nothing.

'That clock must be with me before the show ends,' snarls Red Coat Man, 'or there will be such trouble. I'll search every caravan. I'll search every box and every stable. The person who did this – or creature either – out they will go. I hope they starve!' he says.

Red Coat Man is not a nice man I see. Now he is so angry he has forgotten how to smile. But smile he must, because the crimson curtains are pulling back. The crowd is waiting.

Red Coat Man stares at the gap in the curtains. He covers his face with his hands. He stretches his mouth. He waggles his eyebrows. He breathes quiet a moment. Then he lifts his head. He is smiling from ear to ear. His teeth flash. His eyes sparkle. He strides off through the open curtains.

'Welcome!' he cries, 'Welcome!' The crowd roars back.

'He is a showman, that man,' says Grey Elephant almost to herself.

'He is a cross man too,' says I, 'I would not want to be around when he finds his clock!'

But there is no more time for talking. Out step the golden horses into the ring. Out go the clowns and the jewelled coach. Out I go and Dingo Dog Man. The show begins. As it always does.

But not quite as always. Not quite. As I trot round the ring with the parade I see a man in the front row with a dark cap on his head. He is not smiling like all the rest. He is staring at me. Dingo sees him too. 'Oh ho' says Dingo Dog Man as we run back through the curtain. 'Maybe tonight is trouble night. I do not like the look of him. Not one little bit.'

It is trouble night all right. Outside the curtains Red Coat Man paces to and fro and mutters to himself. But the show goes on. The Silver Twins glide and soar above us. Jezzaralda tumbles and swings and somersaults. The Clowns play all their tricks.

Then it is my turn. I trot into the ring. I run and jump. I walk and leap. But not so quick as usual. I am not as I should be for this work.

And all the time the man in the front row stares.

At last I face the fire. I growl. I leap and through I go. But I jump too low. I almost fall. I only just escape the flames.

And right there, in mid leap, there is a flash. The

man is standing. He has a little box between his hands. It has flashed at me.

'Oh no!' roars Dingo Dog Man. 'No photographs! That is the rule. Give that camera here!' He strides towards the man. The crowd stops clapping. Everyone stares.

'No way!' shouts the man right back at him. 'This is the evidence,' says he. 'You are a cruel man. This dog will not jump the flames again. The police will close you down if you make him!'

The crowd begins to roar. But not so happy as before. 'Cruel!' the people shout. 'Yes it is. It is. Stop it now!'

'And do not think you can start again when you move on!' shouts the man. 'We have reported you. You will be watched!'

Dingo does not know what to do. He looks this way and that. At last he scurries back across the ring and out through the red curtains. And me after him. The crowd is shouting and roaring.

Red Coat Man has heard it all. 'This is bad luck,' he growls. 'I thought we had got away with it you know. We cannot chance it again. You must think of another trick, Dingo.' The crowd shouts again. 'Someone must go out there to calm that lot down – and quick too! Jezzaralda!' he roars. 'Another turn from Jezzaralda! That will do it!'

Mary Anne slips forward. 'I will get her,' says she. 'I know she is ready.' And quick as quick here is

Jezzaralda. She smiles her yellow smile and steps out through the curtains.

'Jezzaralda!' the people shout. They have forgotten about me.

The cats are cross as cross. 'This is worse than ever,' they hiss. 'Now Jezzaralda is on her own. No Twins at all. But soon it will be different!' They glare at me.

Red Coat Man is striding to and fro. 'It is all wrong tonight,' he mutters to himself. 'It is a bad night for us all. I will be glad when we move on!'

Then from the darkness outside the tent there steps a silver figure. In one hand it carries a golden dish. In the other it holds the ticking clock. 'Is this what you have lost?' asks the Silver Twin.

Red Coat Man stops pacing for a moment. Then he begins to roar. He roars so loud that out in the ring Jezzaralda almost misses her hold. 'You are the thief!' he shouts at the Silver Twin.

'Do not be silly,' says she. 'Would I bring it here if I had pinched it? I found it when I went to feed my cattykins. It was under this bowl!'

A silence falls. All eyes go to the clock, to Red Coat Man, to the Silver Twin.

Silence. Then into the silence cuts a catty howl. A howl of rage. Out of the carriage leap Cat One and then Cat Two. They jump high onto the shoulders of the Silver Twin. 'There! There! Him!' they scream. They point their soft paws at me. 'He is the thief! That bad thieving dog there. He planned to run away and take the clock with him!'

Of course no one understands what they say except the Silver Twin because the cats are speaking animal-talk. But the Twin understands. She turns her eyes to each of the Cats in turn. 'Why does he want the clock?' asks she. 'What can a dog do with a little clock like this?'

The two cats think a moment. Then they come up with something really clever. 'He is not a stray at all,' they yowl. 'His person is waiting for him. He has an accomplice! He came into this circus to steal! He is a thieving bad dog he is! He is! He is!'

The Silver Twin stares at me. Her eyes are hard. 'He came to steal? What a wicked dog!' says she. Of course everyone hears this, they understand this. They stare at me and at the cats. They do not know what to think.

'What have your cats told you?' yells Dingo Dog Man. He is not pale now but almost as red as Red Coat Man.

'Explain! Explain!' roars Red Coat Man. 'That little dog is all trouble! Tell us what he has done!'

They all wait to hear. But not I! Oh No.

I run.

I dart through people's legs, past wheels, past caravans. I skim away over the dark ground. I flash through the night like a golden star. I skid up to the kennels where Suky lies.

'Suky!' I cry. 'Up, now, and away! It has all gone wrong! We must run now!'

She opens her eyes. She scrambles out of her kennel. 'But Nip,' says she, 'we have not had our dinners. And you are in your suit. We cannot go now.'

'Now!' I cry. 'It is now!'

I hear the thud of feet. I hear the cries of people after me. Above it all I hear the cats chanting 'Find him, seize him, catch the thief!'

Suky's ears flick forward. She hears it all. 'Now it is!' says she. We leap away through the dark. We skim around the corner. Just in time. The crowd surrounds the kennels. 'They have fled,' yowls Cat Two.

'After them!' cries Cat One.

'This way,' calls the Silver Twin. She has seen my golden coat flash in the starlight.

But we are running fast now. Running swift and steady. We run past the caravans. We run past the fence and over the road. We run into far fields and beyond. We run on, and on again. We run for our lives.

CHAPTER 7

We run for our lives. If they catch us I will be put in chains and Suky will be left alone in the cold streets. So we run until the Circus and the town are far away. As we run, the night is all around us. We keep away from lights and noise. Cars roar in the distance. House windows shine far off. Each time we see a light, we turn into the dark.

Sometimes we pause and let our breath come quiet. In that silence my ears prick up. For I hear a new noise, a kind of scuffling noise, far off. 'What is that?' I whisper to Suky.

'I do not know what it is,' says she. 'But it is far away. Let us run on.' So we do.

We run over flat meadows and along muddy lanes, over furrows and through hedges. At last we stand in the middle of a broad dark field. In front of us the sky rises darker than ever.

'Trees,' says Suky. 'Trees.'

She is right. I hear the whispering of the leaves.

'Trees mean shelter,' says I. 'Let us find a place to rest.'

Just as I step forward, I hear the noise again. A kind of scrabbling, crashing noise. It is closer now, and to one side, where small trees mark a hedge line.

'What can it be?' says Suky. She turns her head. Her ears stand tall to catch every sound. 'It is not people, that's for sure. Could it be a squirrel in those trees?'

No, thinks I. No squirrel makes a noise like this. My heart beats cold. 'Run fast,' I whisper, 'into the wood. Let us hide.'

I leap forward. My golden suit gleams bright in the moonlight. My breath comes short. Suky sweeps ahead like a pale shadow over the ground.

Into the wood we go. We leap through leaves. We crawl under branches. We find a spiky thorn bush low to the ground. We cower there behind fronds of wet bracken. We wait in the thick dark.

Now we hear the sound so clear. A crackling rushing sound. It is high above our heads. Something is hurtling through the branches towards us. We hear its breathing.

My heart beats so loud I cannot speak. Suky pants with fear beside me.

'Halloooo!' a great hoarse voice cries out above us. 'Come out! Come out, my frightened friends! Come out and see an ape in a jungle! Tee hee! Tee hee!'

It is Jezzaralda. She crashes down through the branches onto the wet earth. She lands on soft big feet.

'Jezzaralda!' I whisper. 'You frightened us so.'

'I did! I did!' she sings out in her croaky husky voice, 'but do not fret now, it is nothing to fear. It is me. Me free!' and she laughs a great ape laugh.

Then she waves her long arms over her head, and sets her flat feet onto the wet leaves, and begins to dance round in a circle. Every so often she lifts her big head and sings up towards the dark tree tops 'Free! Free! Wild and free!'

It is a bit like the circus, that is what I think. There is a ring of grass between the dark trees like the circus ring. The moon shines down like a spotlight. A bit like the circus but not much. There is no one cheering here. There is no clapping and laughter. Here it is cold and windy, and dark and silent.

'Why have you come?' says I to Jezzaralda when she pauses for breath. 'And why are you so jolly? Why do you want to be in the wild wood?'

'A wood?' says Jezzaralda. 'No, no, it is not a wood.

It is the jungle!' Her eyes shine like bronze in her dark face. Her big teeth gleam in the half light. 'The wild jungle! I am a wild ape from the wild jungle and I am here at last. That is what,' says she.

'Ummm,' says I.

'This must be a jungle,' says she after a moment. 'Must be. It is green and full of leaves and wet and wild. My mother told me,' says Jezzaralda.

'I do not think this is a jungle,' says I. 'This is a wood. I am sure it is.'

Jezzaralda waves her big head this way and that. She peers about her in a sad sort of way. 'My mother said a jungle was warm,' says she, 'warm and steamy. This is cold and windy. Maybe, maybe, you are right.'

'Jungles are far away I think,' says I, 'and not perhaps in this country.'

'Oh,' says Jezzaralda. She looks cast down a moment but not for long. 'Never mind,' says she. 'If it is not a jungle, it is surely wild. And I am a wild ape and here I am!' She starts dancing once more and humming low under her breath.

Suky is standing on the edge of the clearing. She stands silent and still, and sniffs the wind. 'I am hungry,' says she. 'I do not care if this is a wood or a jungle. I must eat. I shall find something to hunt, something to eat.' She slips under a branch and disappears.

Jezzaralda and I look at each other. 'I am hungry too,' says Jezzaralda.

'And me,' says I. 'But Jezzaralda, I am stuck inside this silly suit. Please can you help me with your clever hands? Unless you help me I am stuck for ever!'

Jezzaralda steps forward and peers at the suit. She bends her head and sniffs along my back where all the buttons are. Then she reaches forward and runs her thick fingers along the button tops. 'Well,' says she. 'I can undo each one. But I need light for that. We would have to wait for the daylight to come.' I slump a bit. I do not want to be a golden dazzling doggo for hours more.

'Or,' says Jezzaralda, 'I can tear them all off with my big teeth. If you don't mind my dear,' says she. 'It may be a bit rough.'

'What is rough to me?' says I. 'I have jumped through flames and run through the dark night. Please tear them Jezzaralda.'

Jezzaralda leans forward. She curls back her thick lip and bares her huge yellow fangs. She seizes the back of my coat in her teeth. She snaps back her head and flicks me off my feet.

I am like a rat in a dog's mouth. I hang waving in mid-air. She shakes me once. Then twice. Ping! goes button one. Ping! goes button two. Then Zing! all the buttons go one after the other. The suit tears open down the back.

I fall through the air and land with a thud. The suit falls about me like a golden puddle upon the ground. I step out of the four feet holes.

'Free,' I whisper to myself. 'Free of gold suits, and flames, and clapping, and cruel cats, and cages. Free.' Then out loud I say 'Thank you Jezzaralda. You are a true friend.'

Just then there is a rustle in the bushes. Round spins Jezzaralda but it is only Suky and Suky has a rabbit in her mouth. It hangs from her teeth as floppy as you could wish.

Suky drops it to the ground. 'Dinner,' says she.

It is sad for the rabbit I suppose. Of course it is. But it is good for us. I have not eaten for a long day now and nor has Suky. She and I lean our heads forward. We eat silent and quick, until our stomachs are round and full and there are only a few rabbit bones left upon the ground.

Jezzaralda watches us. 'That red stuff is not for me,' says she. 'I need fruit and green leaves. Perhaps these trees will do.' She reaches into the dark branches and grabs a leaf. One munch is enough.

'Paah!' she cries and spits it out. 'That will not do at all.'

'I saw some berries on my way,' says Suky. 'The same kind that Mary Anne picked from the bushes by the circus gate. They are safe. We know they are.'

'Mary Anne,' says Jezzaralda, suddenly sad. 'She will worry so. She has always been so kind to me. I did not want to leave her. But I wanted an adventure you know and to see a jungle. I hope she understands!'

I am sitting by the white rabbit bones, full up and

contented as any dog could be in a dark cold wood. 'Mary Anne seems a good person,' says I, 'so why does she stay at the Circus? Red Coat Man and Dingo are not good at all!'

'She knows that,' says Jezzaralda. 'She stays for me. There are not so many places for an ape to live after all. And I love the swinging and the flying and the cheers you know!'

'Yes,' says I. 'Even I liked the cheers, if I could forget about the flames. But I could not.'

'If Red Coat Man and Dingo would go, the others are not so bad, that is what Mary Anne thinks. Even the Twins are not so bad,' says Jezzaralda, 'except I tease them so.' And she shakes her head and smiles all at the same time.

Then she thinks of food again. 'Show me where you found the berries,' she says to Suky and Suky leads her off.

When at last they come back, Jezzaralda has dark berry stains about her mouth and she is smiling. 'They were good,' says she. 'Now is sleep time.'

Jezzaralda plops down. She leans her back against a tree and stretches out her legs upon the dark grass. Suky curls up against her on one side and I curl up on the other. The wind sighs over us and the stars shine down. We sleep at last.

I wake up in the cold dawn light. My fur is wet. A thin rain is falling through the trees. There are shining drops all over Jezzaralda's red hair.

I stand up on my four short legs. Jezzaralda stirs but does not wake. Suky opens her eyes and blinks up at me. Then she sighs and drops her head and sleeps on. Rain stands wet on her long nose and runs in little rivers down her soft ears.

'Uuugh!' I shiver. I step apart. Then I shake as hard as I can. The water drops fly off and I am almost dry again. 'I will explore,' says I to myself. 'It is a whole night since my dinner. Perhaps I can look for some breakfast!'

So off I trot. I must not get lost, that I know. I track my way by smells. I sniff carefully at a big tree trunk and then a pile of leaves and further on a line of a broken twigs. I will know my way back.

Other creatures live here. That is plain from step one. Rabbits are everywhere of course. They see me coming through the tree trunks and scatter to their holes. Their white tails flash in the early light. Rabbits yes. But what else? Above my head I hear a scuffle and a cross voice calling. Squirrel. And once I see a whisk of red tail and pointed ears. Fox trots away on his own Fox business.

Then I freeze. Into the air rises a bark. A bark. There is a dog in the wood. Or is there? The bark come again. It is a bark but it is not like my bark or Suky's bark. Not quite.

I step forward as quiet as my four paws will go. In a space between the trees stands a creature.

He is taller than Suky, yes, but not much taller. He

has four pointed hooves, and two short horns, and tiny tusks that flash upon his upper lip. His fur gleams soft and brown as toffee. He whisks his short tail up over his back. It is all white underneath and shines like a flag amongst the shadows.

He bounces on his four straight legs and tosses his head as if he was dancing all by himself. Then he steps forward and lifts his head. He barks again.

I give a little gasp. It is quiet but he hears it. In a moment he has whisked his head round towards me.

He stares at me. I stare at him.

'If you were not so little,' he says at last, 'I would think you were a dog.'

'If you were not so little,' says I, 'I would think you were a deer.'

'You would be right,' says Deer, for deer he is however small. 'I am a barking kind of deer as you see.'

'You are a dancing kind of deer too,' says I. 'You are so bouncy and so noisy perhaps you would be good in the circus.'

'What is a circus?' he asks taking a leaf of the tree next to him and munching it in his tusked mouth.

'That is too long a story,' says I, 'but you are right about me too. I am a little dog, little and neat, that's what.'

'Little and neat is me too,' says he. 'I do not like dogs much, but you are so little I am not frightened of you. Where I come from, where my father's father

75

came from, there are tigers with stripes. And black panthers dark as night. And snakes as big as tree trunks. And monkeys. So I should not be afraid of dogs in this cold land. But I am.'

'Monkeys!' says I. 'Monkeys! And are there apes too?'

'Yes, yes,' says he snorting through his nose. 'I have not seen them. How could I? I was born in this wood. But my father's father saw them. Big red apes that fly from tree to tree.'

'Oh friend,' says I, 'dancing deer friend, new friend, there is an ape in this wood at this moment. A red ape. Lying under a tree and getting wet.'

Deer turns his eyes to me. They are cold and hard like little shining stones. 'You are a lying creature,' says he. 'There are no apes in this wood. You are trying to trap me.' He is wary now. He jumps high upon his hard toes and sniffs the air for danger.

'There is an ape in this wood at this very minute,' says I. 'I left her dozing. Come and see.'

He wrinkles his velvet forehead and shakes his horned head. 'All right,' says he. 'I can always run away if you are trying to trap me. Your legs are so short, I must be safe.' But then he wrinkles his forehead again. He is not sure.

'You do not know me so of course you must take care,' says I. 'Follow on behind. Wait back in the bushes and see the ape before she sees you. You cannot feel trapped then.'

That is what he does. I trot away under the green branches. Deer steps sideways and vanishes so quick and quiet that I cannot see him though I know that he is there. He steps after me on his hard hooves, always hidden, always following. Watching with his bright eyes.

I scamper on and burst into the clearing. Jezzaralda is sitting up now rubbing her eyes. Beside her Suky lifts her long head and peers at me.

'I have found a new friend for us,' says I. 'Jezzaralda, I have found a new and jungly friend.'

CHAPTER 8

Jezzaralda sits up straight and stares at me.

'I have found a new friend,' says I, 'but he does not like dogs, even little dogs. And you are such a hunting running sort of dog Suky, he will be frightened of you, I know he will. Could you stay lying down if you would be so kind, and be as still as still. Then perhaps he will not mind you.'

'Harrumph!' snorts Suky. 'What kind of friend is this who does not like your friends?'

'A frightened friend,' says I. 'A Deer friend. A dancing jungle friend for you Jezzaralda.'

Jezzaralda leaps to her feet. Her eyes gleam bright. She stretches wide her hairy arms. 'A dancing jungle friend!' cries she. 'Where oh where?'

'Here!' says Dancing Deer. He steps forward into the little glade. His eyes sparkle like stream water. 'Red Ape, Red Ape, I have heard tell of you. I thought it was a far off dream, a tale. Now here you stand in my wet wood. What magic time is this!'

'Little Deer, tusked Deer,' whispers Jezzaralda, 'you are from the jungle too.' She reaches forward one big finger and touches his hard horns. 'My mother told me of little deer with horns and tusks,' says she.

'My father told me of red apes with wide faces and hairy arms,' says Deer.

'Did he talk of butterflies like flowers?' says Jezzaralda.

'Yes, and snakes and creeping things,' says Deer.

'And striped tigers?' says Jezzaralda. 'Oh,' says she, 'we have so much to talk about. Let us go.'

Jezzaralda and Dancing Deer step forward together out of the glade. They vanish into the green wood. I hear their voices murmuring as they go. All falls quiet after them.

'Can I get up now?' says Suky. She is cross I can see.

'I am sorry,' says I. 'Deer are such frightened things you know and you are a fierce and hunting dog.'

She rises onto her long legs and stretches. 'I am a fierce and hunting dog,' says she. 'Hunting is what I do best. I know that now. It is what I am for. That is why I am tall and thin and bendy and fast as the wind,' says she. 'I would like to hunt this minute, but my nose says that all the rabbits are underground. Even I cannot hunt a rabbit when he is under the ground.'

'Perhaps there are other things to eat?' says I.

'There are,' says she, 'but they are nasty. I have tried a worm or two, and one slug. They are not nice at all.'

Just then we hear a noise. Not leaves or branches or the wind or a wild creature. No. It is a people noise. A feet noise. 'Oho, what is that?' says I. 'Hide here with me behind this bush, Suky friend. Something odd is happening.'

My heart is beating hard against my chest. I hear feet, lots of feet. Not one or two people, but twenty, or more than twenty. Can it be the circus folk come hunting us? I creep forward. I peer under the leaves. I listen. I stare. At last I see.

A man is coming through the wood along a path. He is wearing a green coat and big green boots on his feet. He waves his arms this way and that as he walks. Behind him come more people, big and small, old and young, fat and thin. They stare up at the trees and down at the ground, wherever the man points with his hands.

'This Nature Walk,' booms Green Boot Man in a loud voice, 'will take us through the wood from one end to the other. We will see birds and flowers and plants along the way.'

'What about furry animals?' says a small person at the front of the crowd.

'No furry animals today!' booms Green Boot Man. He laughs a loud loud laugh. 'In this country furry animals are rare and hide away. So let us look for birds and plants instead.' He turns and bends down to look at a green leaf upon the ground. Everyone steps forward and bends to look too. Except the little person who stares about him.

Suky whispers in my ear. 'I know two furry animals they would like to see!' she laughs.

'Me too!' says I. 'I hope they are hid away. Perhaps we should go and warn them.'

Too late. Too late.

The little person squawks. He squawks and squeaks so loud that all the people stand up straight. They stare and stare again. Onto the path right in front of them step Jezzaralda and Dancing Deer. They are talking away and have not noticed all the people.

'What are they?' squeaks the little person.

'What are they?' whispers Green Boot Man. His eyes are round like saucers. His mouth hangs open. His hands drop to his sides. 'What are they?' he whispers again.

But Jezzaralda has seen the people now. She stares at them and they stare right back at her.

Jezzaralda taps Deer upon his hard horns. 'We have company, friend Deer,' says she. Then she smiles her wide and yellow smile. 'We have company. We have an audience, an audience!'

'Oh no!' says I in my green hiding place. 'Oh no!' for I have seen that gleam in her dark eyes. 'Jezzaralda is circusing!'

'That is a new word to me,' says Suky, 'but I know what you mean.'

Deer is standing square upon the path. He is half frightened and half cross. He jumps a bit and shakes his head. Then he lifts his tusked head and barks so loud that all the people cover their ears with their hands.

'Oh friend,' says Jezzaralda. Her eyes sparkle more than before. 'You are a friend after my own heart. We will show them a thing or two we will.'

She bounds forward and stops with her two feet square upon the path. She breathes in deep. She lifts her big hands to her chest. Then she roars. As she roars she beats upon her chest with her clenched fists. 'Aaarha aarrh aaarh' goes Jezzaralda.

'Ooooh! Oooh! Oooh!' squeal the people. 'A gorilla! A gorilla!' They cling together in the middle of the path. They tremble. 'Save us! Save us!' they shout to Green Boot Man.

Jezzaralda laughs so loud at this that all the people shake even more. Green Boot Man is not shaking but he is puzzled. So puzzled. His eyes pop from his head.

The little person is not frightened. He is pleased.

'Real furry animals,' says the little person. 'This is just like a jungle.'

'Oh Ho,' says Jezzaralda, 'someone here has his head on the right way. Let us make it more jungly, friend Deer. Let us do it now!'

With a great whoop she leaps up into a tree which hangs over the path. 'Watch me!' she cries and off she goes. She swings, she leaps, she flies through the swaying trees. 'Watch me, watch me!' she calls again.

'And me!' snorts Dancing Deer. He flashes his white tail and off he leaps into the wood. He bounces high through the green leaves. He leaps over branches. He bursts through bracken onto the path. Then off he leaps again.

'Oh giddiness,' sighs Green Boot Man. 'Who would believe this?' Then he thinks a moment. 'I know who to call,' says he. He reaches into his pocket and lifts out a little telephone. He puts it to his ear and starts speaking very fast. All the time his eyes are on Jezzaralda and the white flashes of Deer's tail.

'It is true,' I hear him say, 'here in this very wood. Send a camera man and quick!' Then he puts the little machine away and stares and waits and stares some more. Jezzaralda and Dancing Deer play on.

The people are not frightened now. They gasp as Jezzaralda swings and leaps. They point and cry out when Dancing Deer bounces and barks. They smile and laugh and clap. It is circus time in the wet wood.

Green Boot Man does not have to wait for long.

There is a buzzing in the sky. A flying thing sweeps overhead. It has whizzing blades above it and a glass bubble at the front. Out of the bubble leans a man with a camera.

'Hold on to me,' he shouts to someone behind him in the bubble. 'I must get this shot! What a sight!'

Jezzaralda has two audiences now. She is twice as happy. She grins up at the flying camera man. She whoops louder. She leaps further. She seems to fly.

But Dancing Deer is getting tired. He stops bouncing at last. He spies Suky and me where we hide under the green branches and he trots over to us. 'I am hot and I am tired,' says he. 'This is not Deer work you know. It is fun but now I need a cool quiet place to lie in and green leaves to eat.' With that he vanishes into the green.

Jezzaralda is tired too. And the camera man has enough pictures. 'Off we go,' he shouts up into the glass bubble. With a louder roar the flying thing swoops off across the tree tops and away.

'I think we will just go back now,' says Green Boot Man. 'We can do the Nature Walk another day. We have a lot to talk about.' So the people trot back up the path, chattering as they go.

Jezzaralda slides down a smooth tree trunk onto a big branch. 'It was a great show was it not?' she calls out to us. 'And fun too. But now I need something to eat and a nice rest. I need a quiet time.'

'People will know you are here now,' says Suky. 'Perhaps they will come to find you.'

Jezzaralda leans forward on her branch. The rain is starting up again. She shivers as the first drops strike her fur. 'Mary Anne may come,' says she. 'I hope she does. I have had enough of jungles and cold and wetness. I want to go home.'

'You could go back on your own,' says I. 'You know the way over the fields.'

Jezzaralda shakes her big head sadly. 'I do not want to do that,' says she. 'And anyway the circus may have moved. But if Mary Anne comes to look for me, how happy I will be.'

She drops down onto the ground. Together we trudge back through the wood to our shelter spot. We hear the rain patter down upon the leaves.

'Let us rest,' says Jezzaralda. She closes her eyes. Then she opens them again. 'If Mary Anne comes to get me and I go back to the Circus,' says she, 'perhaps I will be nicer to the Twins. I was naughty to tease them. They are not so bad you know but they do not like to be teased.' She closes her eyes again. The trees drip down upon us. 'I hope Mary Anne comes,' whispers Jezzaralda.

Then she falls asleep.

The rain falls on and on. The light fades. The air blows colder. And at last, Mary Anne does come.

In the distance we hear a gate clang and the sound of a car. A car is driving very slow along the woodland track. We see afar off the dull gleam of its lights. There is a blue light too, gleaming and winking as the car pulls forward, oh so slow.

A door clangs open. We hear quick feet on soft leafy earth. 'Jezzaralda, Jezzaralda!' cries Mary Anne's voice. We hear the tears in her voice and the fear. 'Oh Jezzaralda dearest ape, come out of this cold wood. Come home. Be safe. Please come now.'

Jezzaralda leaps to her feet with a great bound. 'Friends,' says she, 'I wish you good luck. I wish you homes of your own. But now I must leave you. Goodbye!'

She pulls herself up into the sodden branches. She swings away into the dark. We hear the leaves scatter and fall as she passes. We hear Mary Anne cry out. We hear Jezzaralda whoop with joy. We hear the hubbub of two friends meeting after many fears and troubles.

At last we hear the car doors clang again. The car turns round and off it goes. Jezzaralda is safe.

'That is a good thing,' says Suky. 'Jezzaralda is not a woody sort of person.'

There is a rustle in the dark behind me. I spin around and there stands Deer. His eyes glow as the leaves flap and dance about his horned head. 'So my jungly friend has gone,' says he. His voice is sad. 'But you are right. She is not a woody sort of person. A jungle would be different you know.'

'I am sure you are right,' says I. 'And I do not think we are woody sorts of creatures either.'

Dancing Deer turns his bright eyes on me and Suky. 'No indeed,' says Deer. 'You are a good hunter, yes you are,' he says to Suky, 'and you are quick and brave,' says he to me. 'But soon the winter will come. Your coats are not thick and warm. You will not do well in a cold and wintry wood. You need a proper home.'

'Yes,' says I.

'Well off you go and find it!' says Deer whisking his white tail. And with that he skips away into the leafy dark.

CHAPTER 9

'Go and find a proper home.' So says Dancing Deer.
Easy beasy is what it sounds. But it is not. How do we
find a proper home?

Suky sits on the wet ground and looks at me. I sit
on the wet ground and look at her.

'Mmm,' says I.

'Mmm,' says Suky.

'We can't stay here,' says I. 'Deer is right.'

'He is,' says Suky. 'This is no home for you and me.'

'We need people and houses,' says I.

'So we must go and find them,' says Suky. She looks

at me. 'Brave as a lion,' says she and laughs her wide dog laugh.

'Swift as an arrow!' I shout. Then up we jump onto our eight paws and look about us. 'There must be a road near by,' says I, 'because the car drove into the wood. Let us go and find it.'

So off we trot along the track up through the wood. It is dark but the moon is rising and we can see enough to run by. Soon we reach a gate and there we find the road. I push under the wooden bars and Suky leaps over the top. We are on a little hill here. Below us and far away in the dark we see the bright lights of the town. 'We do not want to go back there,' says Suky.

'No indeed,' says I. 'But you know Suky, I think I can see the Circus. All those bright lights on this side of town – that must be the Big Top!' I stare again. 'What is that?' I whisper at last. 'Look Suky! There is something flying this way! Look!'

Suky lifts her head. She stares with her hunter's eyes into the black sky. 'It is our friend! Jackie Daw!' she barks high into the wind.

The black shape twists and croaks and seems to fall. With a rush of feathers Jackie is here beside us. Carefully he sets his feet upon the bars of the gate and folds his wings. 'Oh friends,' says Jackie Daw, 'I did not like that at all, flying at night you know. But I am so glad I have found you. So much has happened at the Circus! I must tell you! After you went, Jezzaralda ran off too!'

'We know. Oh yes we know,' says I.

'But she is back and safe now,' says Suky.

Jackie Daw blinks at us a moment. 'Well that is news!' says he. 'When she went missing, just after you, there was such a fuss! Red Coat Man said we could not move on without Jezzaralda. And he had a row with Dingo Dog Man. They shouted at each other so loud that Grey Elephant had to pull them apart with her trunk!'

'They are a bad pair those two,' says Suky.

'You are right there,' says Jackie, 'but Dingo has gone! He said he would not be a Dog Man any more. He would go and be a Car Man in a garage. He would work with cars because no one cares how cars feel. So off he went! Then Red Coat Man cried and roared and said the Circus would not work without Jezzaralda and Dog Man. But Elephant said she would do a special dance if that would help. And the Twins said they would do another turn. They were wonderful, I will say. They are cross I know, but they were wonderful.' He stops for breath and then shudders. 'But flying at night! How horrid that is. I thought I would crash into a tree. I am lucky to be all in one piece.'

'You are just in time,' says Suky. 'We are travelling on now. We are going to find a place where we can live, a good place, and we are starting now. Will you come with us?'

'I will, I will,' says Jackie Daw. 'I want a new life too,

I will come with you if I may. But I do not want to fly again in all this gloominess.'

'You can ride on my back if you like,' says Suky, 'until the light comes you know.'

'Thank you, thank you,' squawks Jackie. 'I am a brave bird but the dark is too much for me.'

So Jackie flops down from the gatepost onto Suky's narrow back. It takes a while for him to get his feet steady and safe but at last he is ready. Then we trot off along the road, away from the town, into the dark once more. The road is narrow and quiet but that is best for us. After a while Jackie tucks his head under his black wing and sleeps, but making sure his feet grip tight. We trot the whole night through. At last when the first light of morning begins to show in the sky above us, we come to a bend in the road where a green track leads away towards some empty buildings.

Jackie is awake now. He lifts his heavy beak and looks up into the sky. 'If you will stop here a moment, friend Suky,' says he. 'It is light enough now. I will fly up into the sky and look around. I will see what is what and where we are.'

'That is a good idea,' says I. 'And we can rest a while 'til you get back.'

'We can go along that track,' says Suky, 'and find a place to rest.' So Jackie spreads his wide black wings and up he rises with a rattle of feathers into the sky. Suky and I step off the road onto the track and trot

91

between the buildings and across a patch of smooth green grass. We are so dozy that we do not see what is in front of us.

'Oops!' yaps Suky and stops so quick I bump into her tail. 'Oh Nip. Look! Water! I almost fell in!'

She is right. Here in front of us is water. It does not flow. It does not splash. It is still, and it is smelly, and it has stony walls for banks. 'What is it?' I ask. 'It is not a river.'

'It is a canal. I have seen one before,' says Suky. 'It will have boats on it. But I suppose it is very early in the morning and nothing is moving yet.' She yawns. 'I will lie down right here,' says she. And she stretches out and is asleep in a moment.

'That is a good idea,' I say to myself. I lie down and rest my paws and look about me. The canal sparkles in the sun. The trees wave their green leaves above the water and birds hop here and there.

Then suddenly with a kind of chug chug noise, a boat appears around the corner of the canal. It is long and wooden and heavy.

It gleams with black paint and there are bright flowers in pots upon its deck. In the middle of the boat is something like a little house with round windows and a flat roof.

On the boat is an old woman. She has white hair and black eyes and a long skirt made of patches and fringes. By her side is an old dog, big and shaggy. And on the far side of the deck is a grey creature, who lies like a big stone, staring at us from his striped and heavy face.

I nudge Suky with my paw. 'Wake up Suky!' I whisper. 'Wake up! Look at this boat! What is that creature there, grey and strong with his face all stripy? Do you know what it can be?'

Suky says nothing but she is staring too.

Just then, out of the sky, comes Jackie, plummeting down to land upon the ground next to us. He peers with his hard pale eye at the boat. 'I saw this boat heading for you,' says he, 'from high in the sky. So back I came as quick as I could.'

'What kind of boat is it?' I whisper. 'Who are these creatures?'

'I do not know,' says he, 'but we will find out soon enough.' So we go on staring, and wait for the boat to reach us.

Nearer and nearer it comes, slow and steady. The old woman turns off the engine. Slowly, slowly, the boat glides forward. It hits the bank and grinds gently against the stones of the canal wall. The woman throws a rope around a post and pulls. The boat stops right in front of us and rocks quietly on the water.

There is a long silence while we stare at the woman and she stares at us. 'I do believe,' says she at last, 'that you are lost.' I nod my head at this. She smiles. 'Well that is a sad thing but you have had your luck today and met with us. Would you like breakfast?'

Suky and I nod our heads again because there is only one answer to that. Jackie shuffles from foot to foot. 'You may want to stay outside,' says the old woman to Jackie. 'Birds do not like to come indoors I know. There is lots for a bird to eat upon the deck.' So Suky and I leap onto the boat and follow the old woman into the warm narrow room that is behind the little windows. Outside Jackie flutters onto the wooden deck and pecks at this and that until his feathered belly is round with food. In the cabin Suky and I eat bacon and bits of bread and scraps until we are both as full as we can be.

The old woman sits watching us. I look up at her and wonder who she is. 'You may well stare,' says she, 'I am odd I know. People call me the Animal Lady, but my name is Alice. This boat is a kind of hospital, a floating hospital. You are safe here, that is what you need to know. People bring me animals who are hurt and I help make them better.' She stands up. 'Now why don't you go on deck,' says she, 'and meet the others while I tidy here.'

So we trot out through the cabin door onto the deck. We look about us and on one side we see a basket. Inside the basket are two creatures, very small and round. They are as spiky as the sharpest thorn bush. I step forward to look.

'We be getting up now,' says one of them, in a strange wheezy sort of voice, 'so get out of our way,

94

little pup dog, and mind your paws.' Out of the basket they get. They begin to scuttle around the deck, snuffling and whispering to themselves. One of them stops by my feet and sits upright to stare. 'What be your name, newcomer?' says he.

'My name is Nip,' says I, 'and that is Suky over there, and this is our bird friend Jackie Daw. So who are you?'

'I be Tig,' says the creature, snuffling with his nose to catch my smell and looking at me with his tiny pebble eyes, 'and she be Peg. We be hedgehogs to you, young squire.'

'Hedgehogs, hedgepigs, little pigs what dig about the hedge roots,' says Peg. 'There were hedgepigs in this world long before you silly dogs were ever thought of.' She wrinkles her nose at me.

'I'm honoured to meet you,' says I. I step carefully backward to leave them lots of room. I do not like the look of those spikes one little bit. 'May I ask why you are here? I thought this was a hospital and you look so fit and strong you know.'

'A cruel dog bit my nose,' says Peg. 'It is only just mended up. We hedgepigs need our noses 'cos we dig about with them. A hedgepig with its nose chewed up is a gonner,' says she.

'A badger got me,' says Tig, 'just a one as our friend over there.' He nods his head at the great grey creature lying upon the deck. 'Them badgers know how to get us they do, and this 'un had unrolled me with his paw and had his mouth wide to bite, when a dog comes running and away went that badger. So I was saved by a dog you could say.'

'Dogs can be good or dogs can be bad,' mutters Peg. She stares hard at me. 'You don't look bad,' she says at last, 'but you never can tell.' Then she glances over to the badger. 'We all of us have our stories,' says she. 'Friend Brock, our Badger here, was set upon by men with sticks. Alice rescued him, all bloody and poorly he was. The men came after her but she be famous in her way, they knew she would not give up. So in the end they went away and Brock was safe.'

'I was bloody,' growls Brock, 'but not all the blood was mine. I set my teeth in the man who hit me.' His voice is deep and rough. 'I set my teeth in him and his blood ran in my mouth. I remember the taste of him.'

I stare at him. I have never met an animal who bit a person before.

Old Dog nods his head. 'It is all true,' says he, 'but most times it is a quiet life here as you will see. We do not look for trouble though sometimes it comes to us.' He smiles. I see that his teeth are blunt and broken and his whiskers have gone white with the years. 'Alice is old and so am I,' says he.

Suky and I settle down upon the warm wood of the deck and wait. After a while, Alice comes out and goes to the back of the boat and gets the engine going. She unhitches the rope and the boat glides forward over the water. On one side of the canal there are cows in a green field that lift their heavy heads as we go by. Upon the other, tall birds stand in the shallows and watch for the little fish that flash below the shining surface of the water.

The boat glides on. Old Dog sleeps and Brock may sleep or not, I do not know, but he is quiet and he is still. Tig and Peg curl up in the corner of the deck and Jackie perches on the roof, his head under his wing. Suky keeps watch at the front of the boat and I run here and there and look and sniff and bark and am as happy as I am like to be.

On we go. We leave the fields behind and the trees and the cows. Soon we are amongst dark walls, and old houses piled up on either side of the canal. I sit and watch and wonder. This is a town, I know it is, like the one we left behind.

Suddenly I leap up. I sniff the air and sniff again. I tremble and look about me. 'Suky,' I whisper, 'Suky. This is so like the town we started in. Can it be the same place?' I sniff again. 'It smells the same.'

Up she leaps and stands tall and nervous at the pointed prow. She looks, she sniffs too. 'It could be,' says she at last, 'it might be. Oh Nip, Nip, the boat has taken us back to where we came from! What can we do?'

So we stand and sniff and peer and hope that we are wrong. But we have little time for wondering. Something is happening. We are pulling into a crowd of boats. There is a noise of people shouting and calling out. I look ahead and suddenly I see – the canal is blocked! It is closed up with two great doors. No wonder everyone is calling out. We cannot go forward. We are at a stop!

But minutes pass and nothing happens. I see that Alice is joking with the people on the boat next to us. It cannot be as bad as I have thought it was. And then the great doors start to open. Slowly, so slowly, they pull open. There is a man upon the bank. He winds a wheel and the doors go on opening. We see smooth water beyond. Our boat pushes forward between the open doors and other boats come after us.

'What is happening?' I ask Old Dog.

'Why it's a lock,' says he. 'We have to go uphill here and water will not go uphill you know. So we go through one lock then another. They are like boxes full of water. The water rises in each box. The boats get lifted up bit by bit. It is quite clever I suppose but it takes a long time and there are so many locks round here.'

I stare and I watch. We are floating between walls so high that they reach far far above our heads. The doors behind us close again. And then I see that there is water coming through the walls in front of us, through little squares. 'They have opened the sluices,' says Old Dog. 'Soon we will float up and reach the next level.' The white foam pours in and slowly the water rises. We float upon it. Bit by bit we rise up by the high stone walls. Bit by bit we get closer to the high ground above.

I lift my head and yap with joy. I see now how it works. I stare up into the bright sky as we move upwards. And as I look up I see a face above me, looking down.

A face I know.

Jeth.

CHAPTER 10

It is Jeth.

I freeze. I stand like a stone dog upon the boat's high top.

'Well well little lad,' says Jeth. 'So here's the hero dog, the little creep who ran off and left me. You have new friends I see and good luck to them! Do they know you are a thieving, treacherous little cur?'

I stare at him. I cannot move. The boat rises and rises. Jeth's face comes closer. And I see there is someone with him. A woman. She is a round and comfy sort of woman, with fair and curly hair and a smiley face.

But then I look again. That is not right, not quite right. This woman is round but she is not comfy, not at all. Her eyes are hard and her smile is sharp as a knife. My heart goes cold. Jeth has a new friend and she is as bad as him. Maybe she is worse.

'Come on Jeth,' says she. 'Don't start anything. You were lucky to get away with that last job. You must not get into any more trouble. Even if he was your dog before, what use is he to you now? He looks a runty little beast to me. You are well rid of him I'm sure.'

'You are right Bertha,' says Jeth. 'I would not have him back if I was paid to take him.'

This is good news for me. My heart begins to beat again.

'But,' says Jeth, 'you are wrong about me being lucky to get away with that last job. They had no evidence so they had to let me go. That's the law! Tone had run off with the evidence of course. He shared out all the stuff later, fair and square, I've no complaints. But with them having no evidence, I was innocent as the day. Those policemen were cross, how cross they were, but they could do nothing to me!' He laughs long and hard at this.

'Well don't push your luck, that is what I think,' says Bertha. 'If I was you I would be careful for a while.'

'But you're not me,' says Jeth. 'And look over there, see that tall dog. That's Tone's dog I'm sure. Tone is going straight now. Lives nice and clean and tidy and earns his money.' Jeth grinds his teeth. 'Never would have believed it! But his dog now, always a looker she was. We could get a bit of cash for her I bet.'

'We could too,' says the woman. 'She's a nice dog that one, and just the kind that sells. But what good is cash to you if you get banged up for it?'

'We wouldn't get caught,' says Jeth. 'I'm lucky you see.' He is staring at me all this while.

'Well I'm not so sure,' says Bertha. 'The police will be just waiting for you to put a foot wrong. Leave it be and come away.'

But Jeth cannot leave it be. He likes to do bad things I know. He goes on looking at me. 'I have a score to settle,' says he. 'I have a bone to pick with this dog here. He was meant to be my faithful friend and what did he do? Ran off that's what. He let me down. And that other dog too, she got us nicked! I will make them pay!' He laughs his hard and grating laugh.

Bertha grabs his arm and pulls him away. Off they go joking and laughing but Jeth turns his head and looks straight back at me. He winks. It is clear enough to me. He is coming back. He is coming to steal Suky. And he thinks I cannot stop him.

The sun still shines but I shiver on the wide boat roof. I shiver and stare at the place where he stood. I feel as helpless as a pup. Jeth is back. He is as bad as ever he was. And he has found a friend as bad as he is.

Suky has been watching the water rise and wagging her tail at the people on the bank. Now she comes trotting over to me. 'That was exciting wasn't it?' says she. Then she stops and stares. 'Nip, friend Nip, what has happened? You look as if you have seen a ghost.'

Jackie is perched upon the cabin roof but now he flutters down beside us on the deck. 'Who was that?' he rasps in his harsh voice. 'He looked a bad person to me and I know all about bad people, I do.'

'You are right there Jackie,' says I. 'He is as bad as they come. Oh Suky, I have seen Jeth, right here upon the bank, real as can be.'

'Oh no!' she whispers. 'Did he see you?'

'He did,' says I. 'He saw me and he saw you too. Suky, he plans to steal you. I am sure that is what he meant. What a bad man he is, and he has a new friend and she does not look a good person neither.'

'Steal a dog?' says Jackie softly. 'Now that is new to me. But these bad folk can always think of new ways to be cruel.'

Suky has gone as still and frozen as I am. 'Oh no no,' says she. 'Oh Nip how can I be safe? What can we do?'

'We must tell the others,' says I. 'Maybe they will help us.'

'How I wish we could tell Alice,' says Suky, 'but she

103

would not understand us. If only people were cleverer.'

'People are not so bright,' says I, 'and that is that. We must manage this ourselves.'

So when night comes we tell the other animals. We tell them about Jeth and the thieving and the police van and the circus and running away. We tell them that Jeth is back. We all sit together upon the deck and talk of it in the dark.

'I will help, of course I will,' says Old Dog. Tig and Peg shuffle and squeak and rattle their spines. 'We will help you and we will surprise you we will,' says Peg. 'You will see what we can do.' Brock says nothing but growls soft to himself.

'First we must hide away,' says I. 'If Jeth and his friend come tonight, they must not see us. Most of all they must not see you, Suky. You must hide as best you can.'

Suky is a tall dog as you know and she has long legs. It is not easy to hide her. But she tucks up small as she can go, under the bench that runs around the side of the boat. Brock pushes a wooden box in front of her. 'That will almost do,' says I. 'Almost.'

We each of us find a corner where we can lie still and quiet and then we wait. I tuck behind the plant pot on the cabin roof and there I watch and listen. The stars shine down. The water laps against the boat's sides. It is so silent that I hear Vole's tiny feet as he trots along the muddy bank looking for his food.

Then on the dark canal path, far off, I see a juddering shifting path of light. A torch! And behind the light, two shadows.

Brock snorts in the darkness. 'A torch!' says he. 'What fools these people be. What is wrong with their eyes?'

'We are not all like you friend Brock,' I whisper. 'The dark is very dark to me. But then I have my nose. I can smell however dark it is. People's noses are no use at all. I do not know why they bother with them!'

'They have no ears either,' whispers Jackie from the roof. 'What a noise they are making. Every creature for a mile around has heard them.'

'But Alice has not,' says Suky from where she hides under the bench. She trembles as she speaks. 'She is sleeping in her little bedroom there. And she will sleep through anything. She has old ears and they do not work so well. There is no person to help us!'

'I will not wake her,' says Old Dog. 'I will not. I will go inside the cabin now and I will guard her bedroom door and keep her safe. I will not put her in danger, not for you, not for nobody.' He sets his big paws wide and stares at each of us until we nod our heads. And then he slides into the cabin and the door shuts soft behind him.

The torch gets nearer and nearer. And then at last against the dark sky and the bright points of stars we see two tall shapes upon the bank.

'Here we are,' whispers Bertha. I know her voice. 'Now what?'

The torch light flicks here and there about the deck. We all lie still as stones.

'There's nothing on deck,' says Jeth. 'The dogs must be in the cabin.'

'Well I'm staying on the bank,' says Bertha. 'I'll keep watch but that's my limit. If you want to go onto the boat, that's your business.'

'I will,' says Jeth, 'but I'm puzzled. Why aren't them dogs barking? That Nip's a right little guard dog. What's he doing?'

'What are you complaining about?' whispers Bertha. 'You don't want him to bark do you?'

'It makes no odds,' says Jeth. 'There's no one here to listen.'

'Well maybe the little dog's not here. Maybe none of them are here,' says Bertha. 'Did you think of that? I'm getting cold so get on with it or I'm off home.'

Jeth curses a bit to himself. Then he reaches up to his head and pulls his hat down over his face as he always does. 'Keep the torch,' he whispers, 'I've got my own. I'll be back.' Then he steps quiet and quick over the high edge of the boat onto the deck.

He does it well I'll give him that. Quick and quiet and easy, and here he is standing upon the deck and looking about him. I see the gleam of Suky's eyes under the bench. I hear the tiny rustle of spines where Tig and Peg huddle together by the coil of rope. I see

Jackie like a shadow on the roof. And where is Brock? Who can say.

'Why are those dogs not barking?' mutters Jeth again to himself. 'It's creepy that's what.'

He steps quick and quiet to the wooden door of the long cabin and eases it open. Doors are Jeth's special thing and this one is not even locked. It is open in a trice and never a sound it makes.

There is a click and a tiny band of light appears. Jeth has the smallest torch I have ever seen in one hand. He stands there by the door and I see the ray of light pick its way around the cabin.

'Oh ho,' says Jeth in a whisper. Out he bobs again onto the dark deck. 'Hssst,' he goes. 'Listen here.'

'What's up,' says Bertha. 'No luck eh?'

'Lots of luck,' says Jeth. 'The old lady's got all sorts of stuff, nice stuff you wouldn't believe. There's no sign of the dogs. But there's plenty for us here. I'll go and get it right away.'

'No, no,' hisses Bertha from the bank. 'I didn't agree to that. The dog yes, I know about dogs. But I didn't agree to nothing else. Leave it be.'

'No chance,' says Jeth. And back he steps into the long cabin.

Bertha looks this way and that. She does not know what to do. 'I'll have to go and get him that's what,' says she at last. She lurches forward in the dark and tries to step into the boat. But she is not used to clambering about in the dark. She steps, and wobbles and slips and crash she goes, down onto the deck, head first.

She falls. Tig and Peg each uncurl and scramble and scurry over the smooth deck towards her. 'Take this!' squeaks Tig. 'Take that!' squeaks Peg. And both arch their small backs and ram their spikes into her stretched hands.

'Ooooooooow' she yells. 'What is that? Ooooooooow and again Ooooooooow!'

The cabin door bursts open once more. Here stands Jeth but he has changed his shape. When he went in he was tall and square and his clothes hung smooth upon him. Now he is all bulges and lumps. Every pocket of his coat is full of loot and it is so heavy that his shoulders stoop. 'What is going on?' he shouts. He does not bother to whisper. Why should he? Bertha's wailing fills the air.

'I fell and my hands are full of needles,' yells Bertha. She spreads out her hands. They are covered in tiny spots of blood which shine dark in the moonlight.

'How did you manage that?' says Jeth.

'There was something on the deck!' snarls Bertha.

'Well shut your noise,' says Jeth. 'I've struck lucky here. There are gold things, and silver things, and every sort of thing you can imagine, all just standing on the shelf for anyone to see. They are not there now of course,' he chuckles. 'They have found a better home.' He pats his huge pockets and laughs again.

'Anyway,' says he, 'I am going back in now. There is another door in there. There may be more loot to take.'

'No, no,' calls Bertha, 'I came here for the dog and that is what I'll have or nothing. And I cannot see her anywhere. Or can I?' She leans forward. 'So what is that?' she mutters to herself. She has seen the pale gleam of Suky's eyes under the bench, the pale shine of her furry coat. 'Oh ho,' says Bertha. 'I do believe I may be in luck too!'

But Jeth does not hear. He has gone back into the cabin and I run after him. I see him step through the long room. I see the point of light from his torch pick out the inner door. I see his hand reach forward for the handle of the cabin where Alice is sleeping.

There is a rush and a roar and a howl. Jeth drops the light and shouts and waves his long arms. He staggers back. Old Dog has stopped him. 'No further,' howls Old Dog, though of course Jeth does not understand. 'No further. You will leave my person alone. You will go away and leave her safe.' He growls and snarls and barks the words out. Jeth does not understand the words but he understands the growls and he understands the flashing of Dog's teeth.

He takes a step backward. Old Dog leaps upward, as high as his old legs will jump. He seizes Jeth's trouser leg in his old teeth. He clamps his old jaws tight. He sets his old paws upon the deck and pulls. Then he lets go and falls exhausted to the floor. His mouth is full of bits of trouser. Jeth sees him clear at last. He laughs a cruel laugh now. 'Why you are just a silly old dog,' says he. 'No one could fear you!' He lifts his arm to strike Old Dog where he lies.

'No, no!' I yelp and hurl myself forward. I leap up at Jeth. I leap and leap again. I open wide my toothy jaws. But I cannot bite Jeth. I cannot. Never in all my life have I bit a person. And this is Jeth, my master as was. I cannot bite him.

My heart fails me. I leap and I leap, I yap and I growl, but Jeth is laughing at me too now.

'You are no better than him!' he cries. 'You were a no-good dog when you were with me and you are no-good now. Out of my way, you little coward!'

He turns upon his heel and steps toward the open door which leads onto the deck. And then a strange thing happens. The narrow door is filled with darkness, the blackest blackness you ever saw. There is a rush of black wings and black feathers. Jackie's pale eyes shine and his hooked feet reach out with their sharp claws. 'Caaaaaww!' he screeches so loud that the cabin walls shudder. So high that my ears sing at the sound. He reaches with his clawed feet for Jeth's head.

'Aah! Aah!' screams Jeth. 'My eyes! My eyes!' He loses his balance. He staggers and spins and howls and falls, falls with a crash and thump. His head strikes on the table edge. He folds up silent and soft like an old rag doll, and lands upon the floor. There he lies, half curled up, still and peaceful as can be.

Jackie settles upon Jeth's head and folds his wide and feathered wings. 'I have not hurt his eyes. Of course I have not. What a great coward this man is to be sure!' So Jackie goes on sitting on Jeth's head as calm as can be, as if it was an old tree branch.

And now at last the bedroom door swings wide. Round it comes Alice's face. In her hand is an old and battered torch. She flicks it on.

'You know,' says she, 'my ears are not so sharp especially when I sleep, but I felt a thump somewhere. When I opened my eyes, I saw the door was open. I knew something was up! But this!' and she stares about her. 'What a sight!'

She leans forward and peers at Jeth more closely. 'This will not do,' says she. 'This man has all my nicest things inside his pockets. You are brave creatures all of you. I hope that you are all unhurt. We must get this man to the police.'

And there in that dark room she reaches into her deep pocket and takes out a little telephone. I did not think she was a phone sort of person but she is. She puts the phone to the ear that works best, and in a trice she is talking to someone.

'Yes,' says she. 'We are only half a mile from the next lock. I will get moving and you can collect him in a few minutes if you get there quick. He looks very quiet to me. Maybe he needs a doctor. My animals need a vet I know and that is what I care about.'

She slides the phone back into her pocket. 'Well,' says she, 'we must be off and get this man took care of. But first I will go check outside.'

She goes across to the door and steps out onto the deck. In the corner I see Brock. He is panting and quivering as if in fright. I see the dark drops that trickle from his mouth and I know what that must be. Beyond him I see Tig and Peg huddled by the boat side, staring at us with frightened eyes.

I see them. I see the empty deck. I see the empty bank and the dark empty fields beyond.

'Suky!' I cry out. 'Suky, we have won. Brave as a lion Suky, and swift as an arrow!' But my voice falters. There is no reply. I do not see Suky, not here, not anywhere. Suky has gone.

CHAPTER 11

Suky has gone.

She is not here, nor sight nor sound of her.

'I tried,' groaned Brock from his dark corner. 'I set my teeth into that cruel person's leg I did. And Nip! Nip, it was a woman you know. But I bit her just the same.' Brock seems to shrink away into his corner. I see his whiskers shake. 'I could do no more,' he whispers.

'He could do no more indeed!' squeaks Tig. 'Who else would dare to bite a person! He was so brave, so brave! That woman was so frightened! She kicked out with her big boots and shouted loud words. But then she grabbed Suky by her collar and said – "I will take what I came for" – and picked up poor Suky, who is so thin and light you know, and then she stepped back over the side onto the bank and was off!'

'Yes she was off and vanished and all we could hear was Suky yelping and calling out until she went quiet,' says Peg.

'Went quiet!' says I and all the hairs upon my back stand up stiff with terror. 'Went quiet? What do you mean?'

'Well, Suky called and yelped and shouted,' whispers Brock from out the dark. '"Help me! help me!" is what she said. Then I think that the woman must have put her hand round Suky's muzzle because she called no more.'

I sit back upon the deck, so weak I cannot stand. 'Oh Suky Suky,' I mutter to myself. 'I was not here to help you when you needed me most. Oh Suky what can I do now?'

Then at the back of the boat, Alice starts up the engine and chug, chug away we go along the dark canal.

I sit upon the deck and stare out into the blackness. 'Oh Suky,' says I, 'where are you?' But I see nothing and hear nothing. Suky has gone.

We chug chug on and soon lights appear and we see lock gates ahead and there beside them a little house and a police car with its blue light flashing.

'Good, good,' says Alice, 'they have been quick. I was worried our thief would be awake before we met up with the police but we are all right now.'

And so we are. In no time we are fastened up against the bank and two policemen jump on board. They go and look at Jeth who is still lying on the cabin floor. He has one eye open now and has begun to look about him.

'We will not move him until the doctor gets here,' says one of the policemen, 'but he is a sight for sore eyes. He has slipped through our fingers too many times and here he is, caught red handed. It is a fair cop this time,' he says to Jeth.

Jeth sits up slowly and puts his hand up to his head. 'Ouch,' says he, 'that is sore.' Then he looks about him and sees the policemen. 'Oh dear,' says he, 'it is not my lucky day. What went wrong? I am usually a very lucky chap but I am out of luck now I think!'

Alice stands in front of him with her hands upon her hips. 'You have been bad once too often,' says she, 'and I hope you go to prison for a long long time.'

Soon the doctor comes. He is a little cheery man. He comes into the cabin and looks at Jeth's head. 'A nasty bang but you will be fine by and by,' says he. 'We will keep an eye on you. We want you to be fit and well for court you know.' And then he helps Jeth up and they all go on deck and over the boat-side onto the bank. When they have got Jeth into the car, one of the policemen comes back to talk to Alice. 'We will bring you back all your things when we have made a list,' says he. 'But is there anything else we should know? Was anything else missing?'

'Oh yes yes,' says she. 'There is a fine dog that has vanished too. There must have been a second man although I didn't see him. He has stolen the dog! The dog is called Suky and she is beautiful and he could get good money for her I am sure.'

'That is interesting,' says the policeman, 'but it may not have been a man neither. We have had one or two dogs stolen these last weeks. We have our eye on a woman, a clever lady she is too. We think she is behind it. The last stolen dog turned up at the Car Boot Sale. It might be worth checking there!'

They talk some more. But I sit there shaking with excitement. The last dog who was stolen was found at the Car Boot Sale! I can go to the Sale. I can maybe find Suky. My heart beats strong and loud. I trot forward and press my nose against Alice's leg. She turns and looks down at me. 'Oh little lad,' says she, 'you want to find your friend don't you? Well perhaps we may do that. Tell me about the Sale,' says she to the policeman and so he tells her.

When the policemen have gone and taken Jeth with them, we all sit round upon the deck in a big circle. 'The policeman has told me how we may find Suky,' says Alice. 'The person who stole her will want to sell her soon and there is a Sale here the day after tomorrow. It is a special kind of Sale where people bring cars, and park in a field, and sell anything they want. We must hope and hope that Suky will be there.'

The next day the policeman brings back all Alice's lost things and she sets them out upon the deck. There are tiny teapots, little jars and vases, mirrors, jewelled boxes, dainty figures made of shiny stuff. She sets them out in a long row and smiles to see them. 'They are like old friends,' says she. 'I have had them a long long time. They are only things I know, but I am glad to have them back.'

Yes they are only things I say to myself, you are right there. We have all these things back but what use is that? Out there is my friend, lost and frightened, my friend Suky, and no one has brought her back.

Alice looks over to where I sit and seems to know what is in my head. 'Do not worry little dog,' says she. 'I would give away all of these if it would get your friend back. And maybe that is a good idea now I think of it. I could take a piece or two to the Car Boot Sale. It would be a good excuse to ask some questions.' She sits and ponders for a while. 'I will do that,' says she and smiles at me. Then she goes back to her treasures. She polishes each one, and looks at them and sets them out upon the cabin shelves.

When the dark comes she is finished at last. She calls us animals onto the deck. 'Tomorrow,' says she,

'Nip and I will go and seek for Suky. I will take some things with me and pretend to be selling like everyone else. But only Nip and I can go. Brock must not leave the boat, it would not be safe. And Tig and Peg, you are too far from friendly woods here, so please stay too. Old Dog, brave friend, you will stay I hope and sit upon the deck and guard the boat. Will you do that?' Old Dog nods proudly.

'I am sure you will decide for yourself, Jackie Daw, you are a brave and clever bird,' says Alice. 'But for the trip, it is you and I, Nip boy. That policeman told me how to get to the Sale. We have no car so we must walk. It is not so far. Tomorrow!' And she gets up and goes off to her bed.

I turn and trot off to find a warm place by the engine and curl up under the bench. I sleep. I sleep a long while. And then suddenly, in all that darkness, there is a sudden rattle and whoosh of feathers and here is Jackie settling by my side upon the wooden deck.

I am wide awake in a trice. I crawl out of my shelter and on the broad deck it is not so dark. The stars shine down and the moon glows bright. Jackie gleams in the moonlight. 'This is not my time,' says he. 'I am not a night-time bird. But it is beautiful,' and he looks up at the great sky and all its lights.

I look up too. 'It is true,' says I, 'the sky is beautiful, but you did not wake me to look at stars, I am sure of that.'

'No,' says Jackie, 'I have been thinking. Tomorrow,' says he, 'you go to seek your friend. Just you and Alice. A little dog and an old woman. It will not do you know.'

My heart sinks. 'You think we cannot find her, the two of us?' says I.

'It will be hard,' says Jackie. 'It will be like the Circus Field I think. Lots of cars, lots of people, lots of places to hide things. It is hard if you are on the ground. You need eyes in the sky.'

'Well that is grand,' says I, 'but I am not a flying dog you must have noticed.'

Jackie clicks his heavy beak crossly. 'I know, I know,' he snaps. 'What I mean is that you need us birds on your side. We feathered things, we are the ones you need.'

I stare at him. 'What do you mean? I do not understand.'

'Well,' says he, 'at first light I will be off to find friends who can help. Tomorrow as you walk to the Sale, you will see the little birds here and there. They will be watching. And when you get to the Sale, lift your head and look up. I will seek out the High Sky Birds, who will hover far above you. They will help us I know. They will look out for Suky and nothing can be hid from them. They will find her if she is there and they will tell you. Trust me.'

His pale eyes gleam and glint in the moon light. He raises the grey feathers on his neck like a great ruff about his head. 'We will find her if it takes every bird in this land to do it,' he hisses into the dark.

'Thank you, thank you,' is all I can say. And then he lets his feathers fall and shakes his head sadly. 'Poor Suky,' says he. He spreads his wings and half flies, half scrambles back onto the roof to wait for dawn.

I wake into bright sunlight and he is gone already. Soon Alice and I are trotting along the canal path to go to the Sale. Or rather I am trotting on my short legs. Alice is walking in an up and down lurchy sort of way because she is old and her legs do not work quite as they should. But we get along fast enough. In no time at all we are at the end of the path and turning off onto a red-brick bridge. Just as we turn up the steps to the bridge a small brown bird flutters out of the bushes next to us. She lands upon the ground quite close to us and bobs her head. Alice stops a moment. 'Jenny Wren,' says Alice. 'I always like to see a wren.' And then she turns to go upon her way.

I stop and look harder. Jenny Wren hops closer. She sets her bright and beady eye upon me. 'Nothing yet. No sign yet,' she chirps in her high tinny voice. Then she turns her head and peers up into the sky above us. I look up too. High high above, far into the blue, is a shape, a shadow in the sky, floating upon wide wings. Then another and another. 'The big Sky Birds are searching the field,' says she, 'and little Kestrel will be there too, to be your messenger. We are all watching!'

And with that she spreads her round wings and disappears into the bushes.

'Come on Nip, do not lag so,' calls Alice and I scurry after her. But now I remember to look about me. I see a blackbird huddled by a chimney stack who opens his golden beak as we go by and squawks to us. And a collared sparrow who digs in the dust by the roadside and chirps 'No news' to us as we go by.

We travel on and after a while we reach a road full of cars. We go along the roadside on a narrow pavement until we reach a wide gate. All the cars are turning here into a lane that leads into a big field. Alice pays her money to the man at the gate and in we go.

There are cars everywhere and people too. Some of the cars have little tables set up next to them and people are putting out all kinds of things upon the tables; big things and little things, shiny things and dark things, soft things and hard, all to sell says Alice.

'We must find somewhere for me to rest a while' says she, 'and then we will start looking.' She finds a low bench beside the fence. 'I will stop here a moment.' Her face is sad. 'It will not be easy. Suky may not be here at all. I will look. I will ask questions, and I will try to sell my things and hope to hear some news. But it will not be easy.'

My heart sinks. She is old and not so strong. This is a big and noisy place. It is up to me, that is clear enough.

I push my nose into her hand and wag my tail. I hope she understands. And then I turn away and off I go. Off across the muddy field, under the cars, between the people, here and there, sniffing and looking and listening as hard as ever I can.

What a place this is! There are cars parked everywhere and more people than I have ever seen. They talk and laugh and shout and make such a din that my head spins. And the smells! There are more smells than I have ever smelt before. People smells and food smells and drink smells and car smells.

'This will not do Nip my lad,' says I to myself. 'You are a clever thieving watch-out dog. You must stand still as you know how, and you must listen.'

I step quiet to the edge of the field. I try to shut my nose to all the smells. I try to shut my eyes to all the brightness and the bustle. I try to shut my ears to all the din. I stand still as a stone and I listen for Suky.

My ears stand tall and pointed on my head. My breath goes soft and quiet in my throat. I listen as hard as ever I can and at last, at last, I hear what I am listening for. It is a yelp, cut short. The kind of yelp a dog makes when someone kicks it or someone frightens it. A yelp, then nothing.

'Suky,' I whisper and my heart rises full of joy. 'Suky, dear Suky, you are here.' For that yelp was enough. I have been with Suky a long long time and

I know every bark and yelp she makes. And that yelp was Suky.

But where is she?

I am a little dog. I can hide, I can dodge. But I cannot see too well. I am too low down.

I cannot see but others can. I raise my pointed nose and stare up into the wide blue sky.

Up high, higher than I can see almost, are the Sky Birds. They float and soar upon the wind, they turn and turn again in great circles far above the field.

And suddenly they see something, I am sure. One of them checks his turn and bends his head and utters a strange cry, high and loud.

At the sound a smaller bird appears, with bent and pointed wings, bright-eyed and sharp-beaked, swooping over the cars. 'That must be Kestrel,' thinks I. She darts here and there. She stops and hovers like a moth, she darts and peers, and peers again. Then she claps her wings and flies straight up into the sky. She screams as she goes and one person or two look up. But it is nothing but a bird and so they look away again and go about their business.

But I watch. Kestrel screams out her strange cry again. Others are coming now. A barred Hawk rises from the hedgerow and flaps across the ground. A black Crow, bigger than Jackie Daw, hops over the car roofs, peering and searching as he hops. What are they seeking? Who do they look for?

123

Suddenly I know. They are looking for me! They have news for me!

I leap up onto my four legs. I lift my head and bark. Once, twice, three times. Loud and clear. And here comes Kestrel swooping near and hanging in the air above me. 'Are you the searcher dog?' she calls.

'Yes yes,' I bark.

'This way, this way!' Up above my head she flies and the Hawk with her, swooping this way and that over the busy crowd, while I follow.

'This is the place!' shouts Kestrel. She claps her wings and soars away up into the sky. The barred Hawk circles a moment, then flaps low and easy to a tree nearby and watches.

So what is there to see?

I crouch under a van between two broad wheels and I stare.

We have come to the far corner of the field. In front of me is a red and shiny car, and next to it is a red and shiny box. Next to the box stands Bertha, smiling and bright as if she was a good person which she is not. She has her leg in bandages, all stiff and white. I smile at this. 'Oh Brock,' I whisper to myself, 'how happy you would be to see that. You have set your mark on her to be sure.'

Just then she goes to the back of the red van and leads out Suky! It is she, brushed and washed and combed and as smart as a dog can be. She stares about her in a dazed sort of way.

Bertha lifts her up onto the box and there Suky stands while all the people stare.

CHAPTER 12

So there is Suky on the high box and Bertha smiling next to her.

'Ladies and gentlemen,' says Bertha, pointing to Suky and then staring round the crowd. 'This dog has a sad story, a sad sad story.' She stares around the crowd again and makes her face go all sad too. 'The owner of this lovely dog was an old lady, a dear old lady, a kind old lady, who lived on a boat on the canal. Sadly that old lady died!'

'Goodness me!' I say to myself. 'She was not dead when I last saw her!'

But Bertha goes on. 'Now this poor dog, this beautiful dog, is all alone in the world. She needs a home. She needs someone to love her. But, ladies and gentlemen, we cannot just give her away. Oh no. That would be wrong.' She shakes his head at this. 'The person who deserves this beautiful dog, pedigree mind you, will want to pay what she is worth.'

She smiles round the audience with the sort of smile that makes you think of icicles and sharp knives. 'So, ladies and gentlemen, where will we start with the bidding? A hundred pounds? Is that enough to bid for such lovely creature? No, I don't think so. It would be an insult. Two hundred pounds! The bidding starts at two hundred pounds. Any advance on two hundred pounds?'

Suky is staring about her with strange empty eyes. And she stands so still, so quiet. Bertha has given her something, I think, some medicine which has made her like this.

Suky's eyes drift this way and that, as if searching, while Bertha talks. And then, by some chance, her glance fixes upon the big van above my head and drifts down to where I lie between its wheels. She sees me! Her eyes go wider still, she stares and then suddenly she stands tall and lifts her ears and opens her mouth in a tiny dog grin that shows each one of her pearly teeth.

'Why ladies and gentlemen,' says Bertha surprised,

'look at her now. More beautiful than ever. What am I bid?'

'Two hundred and fifty pounds,' says a voice from the crowd.

'Two hundred and seventy-five,' calls another.

I growl to myself under the van. They are selling her as if she was a thing like all the other things set out upon the little tables. 'No, no,' I mutter to myself. 'This is worse than the fiery hoop of flame. This must stop.'

And before I know it I am out there in front of the crowd of people. I am facing Jeth's cruel friend. I bare my teeth. I growl deep in my throat. 'Let her go or you will rue the day. Let her go.'

Of course Bertha does not understand. 'Goodness me,' says she. 'I do believe you are Jeth's dog, my nippy friend. Ladies and gentlemen, this is another sad story. This little dog here was a good dog once. He is become fierce and savage because his owner was arrested, by mistake of course. And now the little dog misses his dear owner so, and he has turned into the savage dog you see here.' She starts to say something more. But she never finishes.

I leap forward. I set my teeth into the bandage on her leg. That is all I can do. I cannot set my teeth in human flesh, I cannot. But I have thought of another way. I seize her bandage, I tear at it. I shake it with all my strength. I tear, and pull and shake and growl. Bertha staggers, and tries to kick me but I have her bandage tight in my teeth. She cannot move her leg. I pull and pull. She staggers again, her foot slips, she reaches out to grab the box but misses, she reels, she shouts and down she goes.

Then Suky leaps clear off the box. She leaps down and stops and stares about her. Then she turns.

Now Suky is not a fighting dog. That is no shame to her. Some of us are hunting dogs, some are chasing dogs, some bring back lost things and others just love to be a pet and cuddled all day long. Dogs can do anything. But only a few are fighting dogs. Suky has never fought anyone, dog, bird or beast. And she has never fought a person. Never. Until today. Until now.

But Bertha is climbing up upon her feet once more. Bertha is a fighting person, that's for sure. She leans back and raises her other foot and kicks hard towards me. And as she kicks, Suky leaps, in a great arc of teeth and muscle. She leaps right up onto Bertha's chest. She snaps her long white teeth into that frightened face. And Bertha goes back again. Backwards, and down, down into the mud once more.

'Aaaah,' says the crowd. 'Aaaah.'

But it is not over yet. 'Help, help!' shouts Bertha from the ground. 'These are mad dogs. Help me!' And she struggles to rise to her feet.

But before she can get off the ground, there is a fluttering and swooping and rushing of air. A dazzle of feathers and beaks and hooked feet. The birds are here!

They fall out of the sky like bullets. They fall upon Bertha, beating her with their wide and feathered wings. They pluck at her clothes with their curved and fearsome beaks.

'Aaaah! Aaaah!' she screams. 'I am dead. Let me go!'

The people are shocked. 'Help her!' cries one. 'Help that poor lady!' yells another. But before anyone can move again, the birds draw off. Bertha is not dead, of course she is not. She is alive and well but she is shaking like a grass in a dry wind and white as snow falling. 'My goodness me,' she whispers as she lies there on the mud. 'Maybe I should try being good. Maybe this bad life is too much for me!'

She sits up and watches as the birds soar higher and higher. Then she shakes herself and leaps to her feet as quick as Dancing Deer. She leaps up and slides away around the vans and cars and lorries. I see her curly head for just one moment in the crowd then she is gone.

Alice is here now, pushing through the crowd, and the policeman is with her. 'Stop that woman!' he shouts. And then he starts to run after the bobbing head. But he is too slow. She has got away. But he keeps running and we run after him.

Then at the far side of the field, we hear a shout and the roar of an engine. 'Stop thief!' cries a man's voice.

'She's pinched my bike!' roars another.

'Get off that bike! Stop! Stop!' yells a third.

Then we hear the engine roar louder.

'Well that's that!' says the policeman, stopping and panting hard. 'If she's pinched a motor bike we've lost her!'

But Suky has lifted her head. She listens. She pauses. And then she takes a great leap forward, then another and another. The crowd parts in front of her and Suky stretches out and starts her hunting run. 'She is after her gazelle,' I think. 'She is swift as an arrow and nothing will escape her.'

I hope that it is true, I hope it very much. In a trice Suky has disappeared into the crowd.

'That woman is getting away, I know it!' shouts Alice. She reaches down and lifts me high above the heads of the people. 'Look little dog,' says she, 'that wicked woman is going to get away!'

I see Bertha. I see her perched on a big motor bike. She is bouncing round the rough edge of the field and she is laughing.

The men running after her are shouting but there is no catching her now.

She turns the wheel at the field entrance and the engine roars louder. She is off up the short track to the road.

But Suky is after her. I see her burst out of the crowd like a golden streak. 'So that is what an arrow looks like,' says I to myself.

She is running like the wind. Her ears are flat against her neck, her legs stretch longer and longer, her back arches and bends and arches again. At each stride she covers a great length of ground. She is like the wind, like lightning, like running fire. She reaches the lane just as Bertha opens up the engine. The bike kicks dirt behind it but Suky has leapt, leapt high at Bertha's back. As the bike begins to roar forward her two hard front legs strike Bertha's shoulders. Then her speeding golden body crashes into her back.

'Aaaah!' goes Bertha. She loses her grip. She sways. She yells.

Suky is over the bike now, tumbling down onto the ground on the far side, but she leaps up again upon her long legs, every tooth showing in her mouth, fierce, and unhurt.

Bertha throws her hands up. She yells again and then she falls, slow at first and then faster, sideways off the bike. The bike, with no one on it now, roars forward into the hedge and comes to rest, its wheels spinning. Bertha lies on her back for the second time this day and Suky stands over her. It is a bad day for Bertha. I can hear Suky's growls from here. And I can see the heaving of her breath under her golden skin.

'Swift as an arrow,' says I laughing with joy at the sight, 'swift as an arrow and nothing escapes her!'

Alice is hurrying forward, still carrying me. We are there in a moment. The policeman goes over to Bertha who is not hurt but very cross indeed. Alice takes me to Suky and sets me down upon the ground.

'You are a hero Suky,' says I. 'You have fettled that wicked Bertha.'

'I have,' says she, 'I have.'

And then there is a bustle to one side and a man appears with a camera and then another and another. 'Stand there!' shouts one of them with a smile to Suky. 'You just stand there, over that bad woman and we'll have a great shot.'

'What a beautiful dog,' says another, 'And so brave. What a story this will make.' So Suky stands over Bertha and the policeman smiles and lots of photographers take photos and people clap and Bertha gets crosser and crosser.

'That's enough now,' says the policeman at last, 'we have work to do.' So Bertha gets up to her feet in a careful sort of way. And the policeman helps her over to the car that is waiting. He has to help her because Bertha is limping a bit on her bandaged leg.

'How did you hurt your leg, love?' shouts one man after her but Bertha isn't saying.

'Good old Brock,' says I to Suky. 'How proud he would be!' And Suky wags her tail to think of it.

And now another policeman is coming up. 'Come and look here,' says he and leads us back to the red car. The back of the car is open and it is full of hutches and boxes. 'We have checked out the car,' says the policeman. 'It is not just the Saluki that was stolen. Here are two cats and a rabbit and a chinchilla I do believe. We must trace their owners of course. But Alice, could you look after them for a while on your boat, until we have found where they belong?'

'Of course,' says Alice.

And so at last we leave the Sale field. We are in a car now, like everyone else. But ours is a police car with flashing lights, and that is not like everyone else. We pull away through the crowd, and out of the gate and back through the winding streets until we see the canal.

'Now it is walk time,' says Alice to the policeman. 'You cannot get your car along the towpath. If you could carry the cats and the rabbit I would be grateful. I will take the chinchilla. It is not far.'

And so as night falls we get back to the boat. And here is Old Dog waiting for us. And Brock lying silent and anxious under the bench. And Tig and Peg uncurling to greet us. And best of all Jackie, blinking his pale eyes and smiling as much as he can with his hard straight beak.

'You are free Suky,' he croaks and his eyes gleam with joy. 'You are safe!'

'Your bird friends found me,' says Suky. 'It is down to you that I am here at all.'

'Well from what I hear, you had something to do with it yourself,' laughs he.

Alice steps out onto the deck and looks about her smiling. 'It is good to be home,' says Alice.

That is what I think too. I start to wag my tail. It is good to be home. It is good to be home and to be safe.

But I am wrong.

CHAPTER 13

It is the next day before I know why I am wrong. It is a quiet day. We sit in the sun all morning and snooze and watch the birds and the flies and the people and do nothing at all.

Later in the morning the policeman comes back to see us and he brings a newspaper with him.

'Have you seen all this?' he calls out to Alice from the bank, waving the newspaper.

She shakes her head. It is a long way to the shops and she has not stirred all morning. 'Well, you are in it and that beautiful dog of yours too,' says he. He steps on board carefully.

'I haven't seen it,' says Alice, 'but I am glad if people know how brave a dog can be. She is a good dog and so is her little friend.' And then she sighs.

'What will happen to them now?' asks the policeman.

'Well,' says Alice, 'I cannot keep them here, I need room for sick creatures. I will try to find a home for them. But you know, it is not easy to find a home for two dogs together.'

'That is true,' says the policeman. 'We find that with stray dogs. Nobody will take two of them. But perhaps the dogs will not mind splitting up.'

'They will,' says Alice and she looks over towards us with a sad frown upon her face. 'They will mind it very much.'

Then they start to talk about Bertha and what will happen to her but I do not stay to listen. I creep away along the edge of the boat until I find Suky. She is sitting high and still and silent at the pointed front of the boat.

'Did you hear that?' says I and my voice shakes. 'Did you hear what Alice has just said?'

'Yes,' says Suky after a little pause. 'I heard. We knew we could not stay here for ever. You cannot live in a hospital after all, unless you are very poorly.'

'It is not leaving that is so bad,' says I, 'although it is. I meant the bit about us splitting up. I cannot bear it! We have been together too long.' I am shaking where I stand. Little dogs like me do not howl but I could howl now like any wolf, just to think of it.

Then I stop shaking. 'I will not bear it,' says I. 'We must not let it happen!'

Suky looks down at me and her eyes are sad but they shine. 'You are right,' she says. 'We must not let it happen.'

'We must go away,' says I, 'far from here and as soon as maybe.'

Suky sits silent a moment. And then she whispers almost to herself, 'We said we would be brave, remember. We will have to be brave again. Maybe lions are brave time after time,' says she.

'Maybe,' says I. 'Maybe they are like us, brave and swift,' and I try to smile. But my mouth will not smile properly so I sit silent and still by Suky's side and think of what is to come. 'We must tell Jackie,' says I at last.

'We will talk to him tonight,' says Suky, 'when everyone sleeps.' And then she lifts her head again and sits once more like a golden statue.

So we wait until the dark is come. When Alice is sleeping and all the creatures are curled up snug, we rise soft upon our paws and go to look for Jackie. He is sitting silent at the very back of the boat. He turns his head when he hears our paws upon the wood.

'You are moving on,' he croaks in his harsh voice. 'I can tell from your faces. It is time.'

'It is time,' says I. 'We must, or Suky and I will be

parted, and the two of us have come too far to part now. We must find a home that will take us both. But what do you want Jackie? I do not think a bird can want what a dog wants.'

'You are right there,' says Jackie and his face is sad. 'I have lived near people all my life but sometimes at night I dream of other things. I tuck my head under my wing and think of flying wild and free. I think of being in a great flock of my own kind. That is how birds like me are meant to live. How wonderful it would be.'

'Maybe you can find what you want,' says I. 'Come with us and see!'

'Maybe I will,' says he looking like his old self again. 'We will go all three of us together and see what we can find.'

'We must go now, at once,' says Suky. 'But which way?'

'Well we know which way the town is,' says Jackie. 'We do not want to go there. So let us try the other way.' He points with his beak away from the canal. 'There is a path goes that way. I have seen it from the sky.'

'Let us do that then,' says Suky.

Jackie makes a coughing noise. 'I am sorry,' says he. 'It is dark. I cannot fly.'

'Of course,' says Suky. 'Hop on my back and off we go.' So Jackie flutters onto Suky's back. When he is steady, we leap over the side of the boat in the dark and onto the muddy canal path.

'We turn through the next gate,' says Jackie. He remembers every bit of the path from flying over it. 'This way, turn here, now straight on,' says he. We go on for a long while, then suddenly he calls out 'Stop! This is as far as I have flown. I do not know where we should go now. But what is that noise?'

It is a roaring thudding growling sort of noise. I tremble a little. If that is a creature with fur and teeth it is a very big. It could eat us up without blinking.

Suky listens. She turns her head to one side and listens again. Then she smiles. 'That is the sea,' says she. 'I went to the sea once with Tone. I liked the sea.'

'But what is the sea, Suky?' I ask. 'How can it make that noise?'

'Come on,' says Suky, 'you will see it for yourself soon enough.' So on we go. It is not long before we reach a town. It is the darkest time of night. The streets are empty. And silent. Except for the pad pad of our own paws and the soft panting of our own breath.

'They are a sleepy lot here,' says I.

'A good thing too,' says Suky. 'We will be safer if no one sees us.'

The road slopes downwards now. With every step the thudding roar of the sea is louder. With every step the salty wind blows harder in our faces.

'Almost there,' says Suky.

We trot across a road that seems to skim a dark

edge. We stop. We peer over. There below us is water. Water stretching away into darkness. Water shining pale when the moon gleams down upon it. And all the time it moves. I have seen ponds, and lakes, and the canal of course. They were still and calm. But this grey sea rises and falls and breaks and crashes and is never still, not for one moment.

'Oh Suky,' I whisper. 'The sea is big and strong and cruel I think.'

'True enough, it can be,' says Suky, 'but we will not go near it now. We must find a sheltered spot to rest. Let us look.'

She leads on a short way until we reach a stretch of grassy ground. 'There!' says she. I see what she has seen. On the dark grass is a tiny building, like a little house almost. It has a roof and windows. There is an open front facing the sea.

'These shelters are for people to sit in and watch the sea,' says Suky. 'It is all just as I remember when I came before.'

We reach the shelter and in we go. It is windy of course. But there is a roof and spaces under the wooden seats where the wind blows less cold. And best of all – food! People have eaten sandwiches in here, and crisps, and nuts, and fruit, and more things than you can think of. And here are little bits of all of them, down here upon the floor.

'Look!' I call to Suky.

Suky skips over to my side. 'Food! Food!' she says.

Jackie has dozed on Suky's narrow back but now he wakes. 'I thought I heard munching,' says he. Down he hops. He starts probing and picking in all the corners with his sharp beak.

We sniff and scoff until every crumb is gone. It is not much but it is better than empty bellies.

'Now rest time,' says I. So Suky and I curl round upon the cold stone floor. Jackie flaps up onto one of the wooden benches by the wall. He shakes every feather then he tucks his head back under his wing. We all sleep.

It is the sun that wakes me. It shines strong through the windows. It streams through the open doorway. I lie and blink in the brightness. The sound of the sea is fainter this morning. I get up and stretch and walk out onto the grass outside. The sea is further off and quieter. Yellow sand stretches so far that I cannot see its ending. The water splashes blue upon it.

'It is so bright,' says I. 'It is gold and blue and shining.'

Suky is up beside me, stretching on her long legs. 'Yes indeed,' says she. 'That is why people come here. But staring is no use you know. Let us go.'

We trot along a grassy strip of land, with the sea and sun on one side of us, and the town on the other. People are out, and dogs too. But they are together and all the dogs have people of their own. Jackie flies with us. He sweeps past on the sea wind. He winks at us and turns to fly above us.

Then even higher, high above, we see a great crowd of black and clacking birds who fly and tumble in the sun.

'Look up there,' says Jackie Daw. 'Look at those black birds playing in the wind! Listen to their noise, so sweet, so loud. They are Jackdaws every one. Oh happiness!' cries he.

He rises into the air with a flap of his strong wings. Up he goes and up again. We hear the dark voices as he rises into the crowd wheeling high over our heads. 'Welcome,' they call, 'new friend, welcome!'

'Goodbye! Goodbye!' he calls down to us. The flock turns and streams out along the shore. And Jackie Daw goes with them.

'I think your bird friend has gone,' says a girl's voice from behind us. 'He has found new friends.'

We turn. We stare. A boy and a girl are sitting on a grassy mound close by us. The girl is short and she is thin. She has bright eyes and spiky hair. The boy has hair as short as it can be and a broken tooth that shows when he smiles. But he does not smile often, I can see that.

'Hello,' says the girl. 'Do not be frightened of us.' Suky wags her tail, very slow to start with, then faster. 'Yes,' says the girl, 'we will be friends. You will see. And you too, little dog,' says she to me.

The boy says nothing but he stares at us. And we stare back.

'Liam,' says the girl, 'I'm sure these dogs are the

142

ones in the newspaper. Do you remember? This must be the big dog who knocked the woman off the motor bike. And the little one is her friend. There were two of them I remember.'

'Maybe,' says the boy. He runs his hand down my back. 'Look, this one hasn't got a collar, Kim. You are strays aren't you?' says he to me, 'and now you have strayed here.'

Kim looks at my bent paw. She frowns. 'Someone has hit you!' says she.

The boy leans forward suddenly. His face is fierce. 'People hit us,' he says. 'They hit me and they hit Kim. We ran away. We were strays too. I hated that.'

'You dogs are like us,' says Kim. 'Your people were not careful with you. Our people were not careful with us, they were not kind. Now we have a new home with good people. That is what you need. Oh I wonder, could you live with us?' She looks at Liam and he looks back and Suky and I stare up at both of them.

'It would be good to have a dog to be a friend,' says Liam at last, 'a real friend who would stay however bad times were.'

Suky and I stand still as stone. We stare at Liam, we stare at Kim. These are friends that we could stay with. We would not leave them. They could be our people and we would be proud to stay with them through thick and thin. But do they want us? Waiting is as scary as watching the flames rise around the fiery hoop.

Liam jumps up. 'We will try!' says he. 'Megan said we could have an animal if we wanted. We will do it!'

Suky's tail begins to wag and I take a deep breath far into my chest.

Kim is up on her feet too. 'You came on the right day to the right place,' says she. 'Now we will see what happens next!'

It is not far to the house that Kim and Liam live in. Soon we are standing at a shiny front door. It opens. Here is a cheery lady with ginger hair. 'My goodness me,' says the lady. 'What a surprise! Come in. Come in.'

She smiles at us. My heart lifts. We wag our tails and in we go. There are two people in the house, the cheery lady and a tall thin man with kind eyes.

'Megan and Dave, you said that we could have a pet,' says Kim as soon as we are inside.

'And now we have found the ones we want,' says Liam. 'They need a home. We think they are the dogs that were in the newspaper last night.'

'I remember reading about them,' says Megan. She stands with her hands upon her hips and stares down at us. 'I had not thought of two animals,' says she, 'but I suppose you could say that two pets are better than one. That tall dog is the most beautiful dog in all the world I do believe. I think she is a Saluki and they are meant to chase gazelle across the desert. We have no gazelle here but we have sand to run on after all. I hope we can keep her. And the little one too.'

'I hope we can keep them both,' says Dave, 'and then we will get help for the little dog's paw.'

But they are careful folk. They do not say yes straight away. 'We must ask the police. We must ring the vet,' they say.

While they go off to telephone, Kim and Liam take us into the kitchen and they feed us. It has been a long night and a long way to trot and we do not stop until we have finished every scrap upon the plates.

Just as we finish Megan walks back into the room. 'Well,' says she, 'there are people asking about you dogs. I thought there might be.'

Kim throws her arms about Suky's neck. 'We must not let them go back to their old owners,' says she. 'Their people were not kind to them.'

'No. No,' says Megan, 'we can keep them, or it seems that way. We will know for certain by tonight. But there are people who are worried about them and have rung the police.' She bends down and strokes our heads gently. 'There is someone called Mary Anne, from the circus, and an old lady who lives on a boat. You know them don't you?' says she to Suky and I. 'Well they both reported that you were lost. I told them they should come and see you here. Then they will know that you have found a home.'

'A circus and a boat!' says Liam. 'What strange places they have seen. How brave they must have been to stick together and come so far.'

'Brave as lions,' whispers Suky to me, and then after

a moment, 'You know Nip, I have never seen a lion and I do not think I ever will. But I know what a lion is like. It is brave over and over, even when things are as sad as can be.'

'And I know what an arrow is like,' says I, 'though I have never seen one. It is swift and true and will not break or turn, no matter what.' And then we smile at each other and laugh our dog laughs and jump up upon our paws and laugh again.

'You dogs look happy,' says Kim and she is laughing too. 'But we do not know your names! What can we call you?'

'We must give them new names,' says Liam. He strokes Suky's head. 'Megan said you were a Saluki. I shall call you Silky. You were born to hunt gazelle across the desert sands, if Megan is right. Well you can run upon our beaches and pretend about the gazelle.'

Kim looks at me. 'What shall I call you?' says she. 'You are a neat and nippy little dog.' I look at her hard. She looks back. 'Is that it?' she says. 'Have I guessed right? A nippy dog. Is it "Nip"?'

I wag my tail so hard I think it may fly off. 'Nip!' says Kim. 'Now you really are our dog and this is your home.'

CHAPTER 14

The next morning I wake up and blink and for a moment I look about me for Jeth's thieving bag, or the circus cages, or the wet leaves of the wood. But they are not here. No. Instead there is a safe home to be in, and Kim and Liam to care for us, and the wide sea shore to play upon.

This very day our friends are coming to see us. First Alice arrives with Old Dog. Dave has taken the car to collect her. Then Mary Anne arrives with Jezzaralda.

'It is a surprising thing to see a famous ape come up

to our house,' says Megan. 'It is an honour. Please come in.'

Jezzaralda is pleased and smiles wide with her big yellow teeth. Old Dog is not so pleased. 'Wild things are tricky enough when they are small,' says he, 'and that great ape has more teeth than I have. I shall stay here in my corner out of her way.'

The people all chat and laugh and tell stories like people do. But best of all, Mary Anne tells us what has happened at the Circus.

'It is all different now,' says she. 'After that big row with Dingo, Red Coat Man said that he was tired of running the Circus and would leave it all to me as long as he could wear his red coat and go in the ring. And he is good at that you know.'

'He is,' says I, 'even when he is angry.'

'So I am managing the Circus now, with one of the Clowns to help me. It is all different, a modern kind of circus. Jezzaralda does not live in her cage any more. She lives in my caravan. And she is even friends with the Twins now, aren't you Jezzaralda?'

Jezzaralda nods her great head and laughs. 'Yes it is true,' says she. 'I am even nice to the Twins. I try not to tease them. The Circus is more peaceful I must say. But I am getting bored with all this talk. Can we go out?' And she jumps up and looks about her.

'We can go to the beach,' says Liam.

So out of the door we go, Kim and Liam, and

Jezzaralda and Suky and me. I look up and there upon the house roof sits Jackie Daw, with his new friends beside him. 'We did it!' he calls out in his rough and savage voice. 'We did it!' and he leaps a moment into the air and squawks with joy. Then he nods to his friends and they spread their black wings and follow us towards the sea.

As we head down towards the golden beach, everyone stares at Jezzaralda. But she does not mind. She likes to be stared at.

Soon we are on the sea shore. Jezzaralda sits upon the sea wall and swings her legs and smiles at all the people walking by.

Suky goes with Liam along the wide and windy beach. She runs in big circles over the wet sand. She leaps and bounds. Her long legs stretch out. She runs like the wind. No other dog can run as fast. 'I do not need gazelles,' she calls, 'I can run anyway. And who can stop me?'

Kim stands by the sea wall in the bright sun. She picks up a long green branch of seaweed. She swings it round and round her head. 'Go get it Nip!' she cries. She hurls it with all her might and almost falls onto the sand. She is laughing. 'Go get it Nip!' she calls again.

Above my head the jackdaws tumble and play in the gusts of air.

The wind blows over us. The sea waves crash behind me.

I leap into the air and bark and wag my tail all at the same time for very happiness. And then I go and get the seaweed for Kim.